The Naked Country

Mundaru, the buffalo man, was puzzled. Squatting on the sand, with fire at his belly and his back, and the meat of the totem making another warmth inside him, he thought back over each step of the trail from its beginning in the high grasses to its end in the river shallows. He timed it again; how many paces a fit man might run and walk while the shadows extended by a spear's length. He added more distance and more time to the calculation to allow for some unexpected reserve of strength in the white man – and was still convinced that he could not have out-distanced them.

Therefore, he must have left the river and struck out to open country. But at what point? Mundaru, himself, had scouted every inch of one bank and he was confident that he had missed nothing.

MORRIS WEST

The Naked Country

Mandarin

A Mandarin Paperback
THE NAKED COUNTRY

First published in Great Britain 1960
by William Heinemann Ltd
This edition published 1991
by Mandarin Paperbacks
Michelin House, 81 Fulham Road, London SW3 6RB

Mandarin is an imprint of the Octopus Publishing Group,
a division of Reed International Books Limited

Copyright © Michael East 1960

A CIP catalogue record for this title
is available from the British Library
ISBN 0 7493 0700 5

Printed and bound in Great Britain
by Cox and Wyman Ltd, Reading, Berks

for
MELANIE JOY

Welcome to a cock-eyed world

CHAPTER ONE

He had been riding since dawn, away from the homestead, eastward towards the climbing sun. The river was at his left, a torpid snake, sliding noiselessly through the swamps and the lily-ponds and the floodplains green with the flush of wild rice. On his right was the fringe of paper-bark forest and, ahead, the gaunt heave of the escarpments, which were the beginning of the Stone Country.

He sat loose in the saddle, long in the stirrup, head bent forward against the glare, his rangy body rolling to the ambling gait of the pony. Dust rose about him in small, grey eddies. Heat beat down on him from a steel-blue sky, parching his lips, searing his eyes, bleaching the moisture out of his brown, leathery skin; but he rode on, tireless and patient, towards the red ridges where the spinifex grew out of the stones, and the wollybutts thrust their roots into cracks and crannies of the sandstone.

His name was Lance Dillon, and he held title, along with a pastoral mortgage company, to Minardoo, newest and smallest station on the southern fringe of Arnhem Land. He was thirty-seven years of age, which is late enough for a man to come into the cattle business and set himself in competition with the big syndicates and the old families who are the kings of the Australian North-West.

Twenty miles behind him, the aboriginal stockboys were fanning out, north, south and west, to begin the muster, which is the yearly prelude to the long trek to the railhead. They would brand the new stock, cull out the scrub-bulls, stringy cross-blooded sires who might taint the breeds – then begin herding back towards the homestead. Lance Dillon was the boss-man, staff-general of this wide-flung operation, but today he was riding away from it, intent on a private business of his own.

To the newcomer, the cattle country promised little but debt and disillusion. The syndicates held most of the land, and the best of it. They had easiest access to port and railhead. They kept priorities over trucking and shipping space. They had first call on experience and man-power, and above all, they had capital – money for pasture improvement, water conservation, transport, slaughter-yards and freezing plants. They could kill their own beef, chill it and fly it straight to the holds of waiting ships, while the small man must drive his steers a hundred and fifty miles and watch his profits decrease with every pound they lost on the trek.

It was a gambler's business and the winnings went to the man who could sit longest on his cards. Lance Dillon knew it as well as the next, yet he had spent his last shilling and mortgaged himself to the neck to buy into the game. He had reasoned long and logically that the only answer for the small man was better bloodlines: stock bred to the climate with its monsoon summer and its parching dry season, resistant to ticks and parasites, growing meat instead of sinew, and hardy enough to hold their poundage on the gruelling drive to the railhead yards.

And this was the reason for his ride to the ridge on the edge of the Stone Country. Behind the first escarpment was a valley, a land-locked basin, watered by a spring that gurgled up perennially from some underground source. There were shade trees and sweet grass, where a new and noble sire could breed his wives in comfort, free from the raids of scrub-bulls and dingoes, untouched by the parasites that bred in the swamp-pastures by the river. Behind the red-brick wall were three thousand pounds' worth of blood bull and fifty first-class cows ready to calve. If his judgment had been right, it was the first smell of success, and he could soon spit in the eye of the financiers who kept him close to strangling point when all he needed was two years without their thumbs on his throat.

He reined in the pony, dismounted and unhooked the canvas water-bag from his saddle. He took off his hat, half filled it with water and held it under the animal's muzzle until the last drop was gone. Afterwards, he held the bag to his own lips, threw back his head and took a long, grateful swallow. . . .

It was then that he saw the smoke, a thin high-rising column, over the saddle of the hill. He cursed quietly, jammed the stopper back into the water-bag, hoisted himself into the saddle and set off at a smart canter.

3

The smoke had only one meaning: the myalls were in the valley, and he wanted them out of it as quickly as possible.

There was nothing singular or sinister in this presence of tribal aborigines on homestead property. All this land was blackfellow country and the myalls – the tribal nomads who lived resolutely apart from the white settlements – had ranged it for centuries. They were the most primitive people in the world, who had never built a house nor made a wheel, nor learned the use of clothing. Their weapons were spears and clubs and boomerangs and implements of stone. They slept on the ground, naked as Adam. They ate kangaroo and buffalo and reptiles and grubs and yams and lily roots and honey plundered from the wild bees. They ranged free as animals within their tribal areas, and the only signs of their passing were the ashes of their camp-fires or a windbreak of branches, or a body wrapped in bark and perched in the fork of a tree. Sometimes, if game were scarce, they might kill a steer or a scrub-bull from the white man's herds, but this was a convention of existence with no hostility on either side.

Lance Dillon understood the primitive rights of the nomads and respected them: but the valley was his own domain, and he wanted it private to himself. His word had gone out to the tribal elders and, until this moment, they had respected it. The smoke, rising above the ridges, was a kind of defiance which puzzled him. More, it was a symbol of danger. A camp-fire might grow to a grass fire which would destroy his

4

pasture in a night. The myalls saw no difference between bloodstock and bush buffalo, and this herd was for breeding – not for blackfellow meat.

The thought was painful to him, and he urged the pony into a lathering gallop which brought him swiftly to the foot of the sandstone escarpment where a narrow gorge marked the entrance to the valley.

Dillon's face clouded when he saw that the log barrier had been torn down and the thorn-bush palisade pushed to one side. Thoughtfully, he walked the pony past the logs and brushwood and inward towards the basin, where the gorge opened out into a small, grassy knoll, twenty feet above the valley floor. When he reached it, he reined in and looked across the green amphitheatre, gape-mouthed with shock and fury.

There was a hunting party of eight or ten myalls, husky, naked bucks, armed with spears and clubs and throwing sticks. Three of them had worked the cows and the calves away from the bull and into a blind corner of the valley. The others were circling the bull, who, well fed and satiated, was watching them with hostile eyes. Before Dillon had time to open his mouth, there were three spears in the great animal, and two men with clubs were battering at his hindquarters to bring him down.

For one suspended moment, Dillon sat, paralysed by the sight of the senseless slaughter. Then, with a wild howl of anger, he clapped spurs into the pony and went racing down the incline, towards the myalls. As he galloped, he wrenched the stockwhip from his saddle and whirled its long lash, trying to cut them down. They scattered at his approach, and his momentum carried him through and beyond them, while the dying bull bellowed and tried to raise itself on its forelegs. Dillon wheeled sharply and charged again, flailing at them with his whip, but before he had gone twenty yards a spear caught him in the right shoulder, so that he dropped the whip and almost toppled from the saddle. Another flew over his head, a third carried away his hat and the three bucks came running in as reinforcements, so that he knew they would kill him if he stayed.

Gasping with pain, he wrenched the pony's head round and galloped him back towards the defile, with the bellows of the dying bull in his ears and the spear-haft dangling from the bloody wound in his left shoulder.

The myalls followed him, running, right to the mouth of the defile, then they turned back to the slaughter of the great bull for which Dillon had paid three thousand pounds.

For the first wild minutes of his flight, Dillon was incapable of coherent thought. Anger, pain, and a blind animal urge to self-preservation, drove him head-long through the gorge and out towards the shelter of the paper-bark trees. He was a mile away from the valley before he slackened rein and let the jaded pony's head droop, while he slumped wearily in the saddle and tried to take command of himself.

The wound in his shoulder forced itself first on his attention. It was deep and painful, and bleeding pro-

6

fusely. The barbed spear had torn through the shoulder muscles and the drag of the hanging haft was an intolerable agony. He could not hope to ride twenty miles like this under a noon sun. Yet to rid himself of the spear would call for a surgery more brutal than the wound itself. It could not be pulled out, the barbs would lacerate muscle and sinew. The haft must be broken off and the head forced clean through his body until it could be drawn out in front. The mere contemplation of the operation made him dizzy and sick. He closed his eyes and been his head almost to the saddle pommel, until the faintness passed.

His thoughts leapt back to the valley and anger seemed to pump new strength into his body. The slaughter of the bull made a monstrous mockery of all his hopes and plans. He was finished, cleaned out, ready for the bailiffs . . . because a bunch of meat-hungry myalls wanted to show their maleness by cutting down the master of the herd.

Then a new thought struck him. They weren't meat hungry at all. The grass flats were full of game, kangaroo and wallaby and stray steers. There were geese on the billabongs and fish in the river reaches. No need for the largest tribal unit to go hungry.

There was more, much more to the killing of the king beast and the attack on his own person. There was deliberate trespass – against the elders and against himself. He remembered that all the bucks had been young ones, sleek-skinned, fast on their feet, aggressive. The old ones understood the conventions of co-existence with the whites. They knew the power of the

North-West police: solitary, relentless men who would follow a man for months to exact the penalty of rebellion. Tribal killings were one thing, but violence against the white man was quite another, and the old men wanted no part in it.

The young ones thought differently. They resented the authority of the elders. They resented still more the presence of the strangers on their tribal preserves. The sap ran strongly under their dark skins and they must prove to themselves and to their women that they were men who would one day rule in the councils of the tribe. They were not fools. When the first blood heat had subsided they would see how far they had fallen under the displeasure of the old ones, and how the vengeance of the white man would fall on the whole tribe. So they would become cunning and try to conceal their trespass.

Then, Dillon knew, they would try to kill him and hide his body, so that no one would know for certain how he had died.

Fear took hold of him again, a cramp in the belly, a cold constriction round his heart. Instinctively, he looked back towards the ridge, to see, silhouetted against the skyline, a solitary figure, trailing a bundle of throwing-spears in one hand, and with the other shading his eyes as he scanned the spreading plain below. Dillon urged the pony deeper into the shadows of the paper-barks and halted again to consider the situation.

Soon they would begin to follow him, tracking him like a bush animal by hoof-pad and chipped stone and broken twig and the ants clustered over his blood-drops. They would circle between him and the home-stead, cutting off his retreat, and if he tried to out-distance them they would find him the sooner, because a fresh bushman could last longer than a jaded horse and a rider wounded and rocking in the saddle.

The river was his one hope. It would break his tracks and water his pony and cleanse his wound. Its tropical shore-growth would shelter him while he rested and, with luck and a care for his strength, he might work his way down-stream back to the homestead. It was a slim chance; but the strength was draining out of him with the slow seep of blood under his shirt. Now, or never, he must make the move, heading southward in a wide arc so that the trees would shelter him as long as possible. The course would take him five miles farther up-stream, but he dared not risk a break across open country to the nearer reaches.

He took a long drink from the water-bottle, tightened the reins in his left hand and, with the spear still jolting pitilessly in his back, set off through the grey trees towards the distant water.

Mundaru, the Anaburu man, squatted on a flat lime-stone ledge and watched the white man ride away. He could not see him, but his progress was plainly marked by the shift of a shadow among the tree-boles, the rise of a flock of parrots, the panic leap of a grey wallaby out of the timber-line. The progress was slow, and would get slower yet, but the direction of it was clear. He was heading towards the river.

Mundaru noted these things calmly, without rancour or jubilation, as he would have noted the movements of a kangaroo or a bush turkey. He calculated how long it would take his quarry to reach the water, and how long more it would take him to work his way down-stream to the point where Mundaru planned to intercept and kill him. There was no malice in the equation. It was part of the mathematics of survival, like the slaying of the newborn in time of drought, like the killing of a woman who dared to look upon the dream-time symbols that only a man must see. Dillon had been a little right and more than half wrong in his judgment of Mundaru and his associates. Their entry into the valley had not been a trespass but a ritual return to an old and sacred place where the spirit people lived. An order to stay away from it was meaningless. It was a place to which they belonged – a question not of possession, but of identity. The ridges which Dillon saw simply as a pen for his stud were a honeycomb of caves whose walls were covered with totem drawings, the great snake, the kangaroo, the turtle, the crocodile and the giant buffalo, Anaburu, which was Mundaru's own totem, the source of his existence, the symbol of his personal and tribal relationship.

The slaughter of the bull was no wanton act, but an act of religious significance. In some tribes, a man must refrain from killing or eating his totem animal. In Mundaru's tribe, the people of the dream-time had set a different pattern. The totem must be killed and eaten, for from this mystical merging flowed strength, virility and a promise of fertility. Mundaru had prepared himself for the moment by taking red and yellow ochre and charcoal and the blood of a kangaroo, and drawing his own buffalo figure on the wall of one of the caves. The intrusion of the white man was, therefore, a violent and dangerous interruption of a life-giving ritual, which must be avenged if Mundaru and his brothers of the buffalo totem were not to suffer in their own bodies.

Dillon had been right when he guessed at other motives; resentment of white intruders, fear of the elders and of the inexorable vengeance of the policeman. But these considerations were secondary and sophisticated, the pragmatic reasoning of men who lived in two times, with one foot in the twentieth century and the other in a tribal continuum of magic, sorcery and spirit symbols.

So, Mundaru, the buffalo man, sat on his high rock in the sun and planned his pursuit and his killing.

First, he would go down into the valley and eat the flesh of the big bull which the others were now roasting over the fire. When he had eaten, he would sit down and have them paint his body with totemic patterns, in ochre and charcoal and the blood of the bull. The others would go with him to flush the quarry and cut off his lines of retreat. But, because Mundaru had drawn the picture in the cave, and Mundaru had thrown the first spear into the side of the great bull, Mundaru must be the one to kill him. When he was dead, they would hide the body in a spirit place, where the policeman would never find it.

To this point, everything was simple and consequential for Mundaru; but beyond it there was doubt and a small darkness of fear.

By attacking the white man, he had taken the first step outside the tribe and into a pattern of existence he did not understand. He had killed before, in a tribal blood-feud. But in this he had been directed and supported by the elders. They had taken him to a secret place and shown him the stone with the symbol of the victim on it. They had given him the feathered boots and the spear made potent by a special magic and sent him off on his mission. When he returned they had welcomed him with honour.

But this was a matter of totem and not of tribe. The elders would be divided. There would be no magic to help him, because Willinja, the sorcerer, was a kangaroo man, and, moreover, he hated Mundaru, because he knew Mundaru coveted his latest wife. In the council, he would speak against him, and if he swayed them, a magic might be made which was terrible to contemplate. But he was committed now and he could not turn back. The spear does not return to the hand of the thrower, nor the blown seed to the pod. He could only drink the blood of the bull and trust to it for strength and security.

Far away to the south he saw a white egret rise, flapping and screaming, and knew that the white man had left the trees and entered the high grass of the swamp lands. He stood up, and carrying his spears and club,

began to stumble through the high grasses towards the river.

By normal measurement, it was no more than half a mile away, but it took him more than two hours to reach it. A dozen paces and he had to rest, head swimming and heart pumping, his body bathed in sweat, a slow blood seeping out round the spear-blade in his shoulder. Each step must be measured, each foot planted firmly, before the other was moved. If he fell again, he might never get up. He was parched from loss of body-fluids – blood and lymph and perspiration – and the first torments of thirst were beginning to nag him. The ants were still clustered on his skin, and from the low ground insects rose in clouds about his face, but he dared not let go the staff to brush them away.

When he reached the river, he saw that it was twenty feet below him, screened by a tangle of bushes and the long tuberous roots of pandanus palms. He had to grope his way fifty yards up-stream before he found a small, sandy slope that ran down clear to the beach. With infinite pain, he eased himself into a sitting position till his legs hung over the bank, then pushed himself off with the staff and slid down on the seat of his trousers to the water's edge.

He drank, greedily, lifting the water in his cupped hand and lapping it from the palm like a dog. When he felt a small strength seeping back to him he worked his way out of his shirt, rinsed it in the stream and then tore it with his teeth and his left hand into strips and tampons which he laid carefully on a rock-shelf beside him. This done, he rested and drank a little more, trying to steel himself to the brutal surgery of extracting the spear-head.

It must be done swiftly or not at all, but his body was weak and his will reluctant to invite a new pain. Finally, he came to it. Summoning all his strength, he closed his fingers round the barbed wood and wrenched it forward. To his surprise, it came free, with a small rush of blood and a pain that made him cry out. His impulse was to fling it from him, far into the water, but he checked it swiftly, remembering that he was a hunted man, with no weapon but the broken haft. He laid the jagged head on the rock beside him, and, using the strips of torn shirt, began to bathe and cleanse the wound. It was long, slow work, because the spear had entered high up in his back and every movement sent a leaping pain through the torn shoulder muscles. He thought of bathing himself in the river, but remembered in time that this was crocodile water and that the blood might bring them swimming, in search of him. Suddenly, there was a new fear: blood-poisoning. A native weapon must be crawling with infection. Sick and hunted, he was days away from medical attention – if, indeed, he would ever come to it.

He sat a long time, chewing on the bitter thought, until he remembered a thing out of a lost time. He had seen the homestead aborigines plastering cuts with spider-web, and someone had remarked that there was a relation between the glutinous web and penicillin. He looked around and saw, strung between the roots of a pandanus, a big web with a huge black spider in the centre of it.

With the spear-haft in his hand, he inched his way up the bank and struck at the web. The spider swung away, hanging on a single filament, Dillon wound the wrecked strands around the top of his staff and drew them towards him. He rolled the sticky threads into a ball and packed them into the wound with a tampon of shirt. Finally, after many failures, he succeeded in fixing a bandage over his shoulder and under his right armpit and tightening it with a tourniquet. It might hold long enough to staunch the bleeding and let the blood congeal.

When it was all done, he felt weary and hungry and desperately alone. He was faced with the simplest problem of all – survival – yet he had only the sketchiest idea of how to solve it. First he must eat, to restore his ravaged strength. If he wanted to sleep he must go, like an animal to a safe earth. He must pit his twentieth-century mind against the primitive strategy of the no-mad hunters. Elementary propositions all of them, until he came to apply them.

Where did the fish run? What bait would attract them to a line? And failing a line and bait, how did one catch them? How did one stalk game, while men were stalking him? What plants were edible and what poisonous? Where to hide from men who read signs in the dust and in the chipped bark of a tree-trunk?

As he sat, sick and light-headed with concussion, ruffling the water with his hand, the nature of his dilemma became vividly clear. All this land belonged to him, but he knew almost nothing about it. He was in it, but not of it. Its secrets were lost to him and he walked it as a stranger. All its influences seemed malign and he knew that he could starve amid its primal plenty.

So he tried desperately to reassemble the scraps and shards of knowledge he had picked up from the aboriginal stockboys and the old bushmen who had lived blackfellow-fashion for months on end in the outback country. There were edible grubs in the tree-boles, lily-roots in the lagoons, yams and ground-nuts on the river flats. A man could make a meal of the screeching cicadas, provided his civilised stomach did not revolt at the strangeness. The flesh of a snake was white and sweet-tasting, but a lizard was oily and hard to digest. The aborigine did not hunt at night. He was afraid of the spirit men who haunted the rocks and the trees and every dip and hollow of the ancient earth.

Dillon's vagrant mind caught and held this last scrap of memory. Here, at last, was hope – a pointer to possible salvation. If he could gather a little food and find himself a hole for the daytime hours, he might build enough strength to move at night, while the myalls were huddled over their camp-fires. The river could be his road, the darkness his friend. But time was running against him. He must act quickly. Any moment now, the hunters might come: black, naked men, with flat faces and knotted hair and tireless feet and killing spears wrapped in bundles of paper-bark.

. . . . . .

When Mundaru and his myalls came out of the valley, the first thing they saw was Dillon's horse, riderless and cropping contentedly in the wild rice that bordered the swamp.

Two of the bucks began moving towards it with spears at the ready, but Mundaru called them back. It was a good thing, he told them. The white man was wounded and now had been thrown. There was no need to split up. They would find him quickly and despatch him. The horse would make his way back to the homestead, or be picked up by one of the stock-boys. Its discovery would lend the colour of an accident to the white man's death.

They grinned, acknowledging his cleverness, and followed him as he walked in a wide arc until they found the point where the pony had emerged from the grass-flats. It was a simple matter to back-track his movements until they came to the tiny clearing where Dillon had lain after his fall.

Mundaru knelt to examine the signs. There was the bruised and flattened grass, the blood, congealed now and covered with crawling ants; but the size and spread of it showed how long the white man had lain there, and how badly hurt he must be. There was a splinter of wood from the broken spear, and a scrap of cotton from his shirt. Under the tangle of grass were deep heel-prints in the earth and rounded hollows made by his knees as he struggled to his feet. As Mundaru pointed out all these things, the others nodded and talked in low voices.

He had stood here a long time. There he had begun

to walk, leaning on a stick. The intervals between his prints were irregular, showing him weak and uncertain on his feet. As they followed them through the parted grasses, they saw where he had rested and where a drop of blood had spilt on the stalks and how deeply his staff had dug into a soft patch of ground. The track was as plain as that of a wounded animal and they followed it swiftly to the sandy slide which led down to the water's edge.

Here they halted, momentarily puzzled, until Mundaru's quick eyes saw the broken spider-web and the patch of sand whose surface was still soft and friable, while the surrounding area was set in a thin, dry crust. He frowned with displeasure. The white man knew he was being hunted. He had begun to cover his tracks.

He stood up and, while the others watched him, walked a few yards up-stream and then down again, scanning the bushes on either side of the water, then the shallows themselves, where the stream slid quietly over white sand and rocky outcrops and pockets of rounded stones. Twenty feet from the spot where Dillon had entered the water, he found what he was looking for: a flat stone, kicked out of its mooring, so that the underside of it was exposed through the clear water. All the other pebbles in the pocket were rounded and smoothed by the rush of water and sand, but this one was rough and reddish where it had lain protected in the river-bed.

Mundaru called to the bucks and showed them the sign. Their quarry was heading down-stream. They had only to follow him, beating the banks as they went.

He was weak and moving slowly. In the water he must move slower still. It was still a long time to sunset and they could not fail to find him.

He waited until three of the bucks had waded across to the opposite bank; then they set off, walking fast, heads bowed and eyes alert, like hounds closing in for the kill.

CHAPTER TWO

WHEN SUNSET CAME, Mary Dillon stood on the veranda of the homestead, watching the shadows lengthen across the brown land, the ridges turn from ochre to deep purple, the sun lapse slowly behind them out of a dust-red sky. It was the hour when she came nearest to peace, nearest to comfort in this alien, primeval country.

The days were a blistering heat when the thermometer on the door-post read a hundred and fifteen of shade temperature and the willy-willies raced across the home paddocks – whirling pillars of wind and sandstone grit. The nights were a chill loneliness, with the dingoes howling from the timber and the myalls chanting down by the river, and Lance snoring happily, oblivious of her terror. But in this short hour, which was neither dusk nor twilight, but simply a pause between the day and first stride of the dark, the land became gentle, the sky softened, and the bleached, neighbourless buildings took on the illusory aspect of home.

It would never be truly home to her. After three years of marriage to Lance Dillon and two visits to her family in Sydney, she knew it for a certainty. She was a city girl, born and bred to tiled roofs and trim lawns and the propinquity of people like herself. She needed a husband home at seven, pulling out of the driveway at eight-thirty in the morning, and a comforting domestic presence in between – not this brown man with the leathery strength and the distant eyes, gone for days at a time, then ambling homeward, dusty and saddle-weary, to demand her interest and her comfort and her encouragement in this bleak ambition of his.

Other women, she knew, made a life and a happiness for themselves in the outback country. They lived a hundred miles from the nearest neighbour, their only company the homestead lubras and the piccaninnies, their only visitors the policeman, the pilot of the mail-plane and the flying doctor. Yet when she heard them talking in the daily gossip session over the pedal radio network, she read the contentment in their voices and wondered why she had never been able to attain it. 'Give it time,' Lance had told her, in his calm, positive fashion. 'Give it time and patience and you'll grow to love it. It's an old land, sweetheart – not old and used up like Europe, but old because the centuries have passed it by and the seas have cut it off from change. We've got birds and animals and plants you'll find nowhere else in the world. The myalls – even the home-stead blacks – are our last link with pre-history. But it's new too. The soil has never seen a plough, the waters have never been dammed, and nobody's even guessed at what's under the surface. All we need is oil and we could explode into growth, like America, over-night. Isn't it worth a little waiting and a little courage?'

When he talked like that, so strangely out of

character for a hard-driving cattleman, she had never been able to resist him. So she smiled ruefully and submitted. But now, after three years, the land was still a stranger, and Lance, it seemed, was becoming a stranger too. He was gentle as ever, considerate in his casual fashion; but he seemed not to need her any more, because she had failed him as she had failed herself.

Soon she must face the question: what to do about it? This land demanded a wholeness. One could not love it with a divided heart, nor fight it with a defective relationship. A rifted rock split swiftly under the day-long heat and the bitter cold of the inland nights. A rifted marriage had as little chance of survival. A man with a discontented wife was beaten before he began. Her choice, therefore, was simple and brutal: make good the marriage promise of submission and surrender, or make an honest admission of defeat and go away, leaving the man and the land to work out their own harsh harmony.

Yet, for all the apparent simplicity of the equation, there was a subtler corollary. Given the submission and the surrender, was there love enough in her and understanding enough in him, to guarantee a permanence and an ultimate contentment?

Three years ago, when Lance Dillon had come striding into her life, bronzed, smiling, confident, a country giant in suburbia, she had had no doubts at all. This was a land-tamer, a man to walk deserts and watch them blossom under his boot-soles; a woman-tamer too, strong as a tree for shelter and support. Now, in another time and in a far country, he looked disappoint-

24

ingly different. The immensity of the land dwarfed him. Its harshness honed the humour out of him, as the winds scored the sandstone rocks and twisted the trees, so that their roots must thrust deeper into the hungry soil for nourishment and anchorage. But if the soil were dry and the root-hold shallow the tree would die, as a man would die if there were not love or strength enough to support him against the storm.

She had loved him once. She still loved him. But enough. . . ? That was a hard question and she could not wait too long to answer it.

She shivered as the first chill of evening stirred in the wind, and walked into the house where the soft-footed lubras were bustling about the kitchen and laying the table for dinner. Tonight was an occasion – whether for cheerfulness or irony, depended on her. It was their wedding anniversary and Lance had promised to be home by sunset.

Normally, he paid little attention to wifely demands for punctuality, explaining patiently at first, and later with irritation, that in the territory no one could possibly live by the clock. It was big country, the herds were scattered. A man could travel only as fast as a tired horse; and horses fell lame, wandered in their hobbles or were taken with colic from cropping too long in the rank river grasses. She must expect him when he came and learn to be neither scared nor impatient and, above all, not to nag. A nagging woman was worse than saddle-galls to a bushman. More importantly, the stockboys had scant respect for a hen-pecked boss. They reasoned, accurately enough, that a man who could not control his woman, could hardly control his cattle or his men either.

But tonight – his eyes had brightened as he said it – yes, tonight was different. He would not go to the muster, but out to the valley, where the breeders were. He would be home by dark – give an hour, take an hour, in the fashion of the bush. Then he had kissed her and ridden off and the memory of the kiss was the one small light in the gathering darkness of doubt and disillusion. Perhaps tonight it would flare up into a renewal of passion, of hope for both of them.

In the dining-room, Big Sally, queen of all the house-women, was laying the last of the silver. She was married to one of the stockboys and her heavy body was swollen and shapeless with continued child-bearing. She was dressed in a black cotton frock with a starched apron over it, but her feet were bare and her broad, flat face incongruous under the white maid's cap. She looked up, grinning, as Mary Dillon entered and said in her thick, husky voice: 'All right, missus. Boss come soon, eh? Catch 'im bath, clean clothes. Eat good, drink good. Maybe this time make 'im piccaninny longa you?' Her big body quivered as she went off into long gurgles of laughter and, in spite of herself, Mary laughed too.

'Maybe, Sal. Who knows?'

The big lubra chuckled wheezily.

'Boss know. Missus know. You dream 'im right, he come . . .'

She bustled out, with a slap of bare feet and a rustle of starched linen, while Mary Dillon stood looking down at the white napery and the bright silver so incongruous here in the middle of nowhere.

'You dream 'im right, he come . . .' The aborigines believed that, in the making of a child, the act of union was only the beginning, but that an enlivening spirit must be dreamed into the womb. Perhaps this was the lack between Lance and herself – the dreaming. They wanted a child, wanted it desperately, each for a different reason; she, because of the hunger for completion, the need to fill the loneliness in which she lived; he, for the promise of continuity, a son to carry on the conquest of the land, push out the frontiers and hold them against time and nature. But so far, it seemed, they had not dreamed right, and soon there might be no dreams left.

For want of anything better to do, she walked to the sideboard and began refilling the whisky decanter from Lance's last bottle of Scotch. Then, almost without thinking, she poured a glass for herself, laced it with water and drank it slowly. It was cocktail-time in the city and this was her ritual commemoration of the life she had left behind. But there was defiance in it too – a small symbol of rebellion.

Once, in their first year of marriage, Lance had come home late to find her sitting by the fire with a drink at her elbow. He had frowned and then chided her, smiling:

'Never drink with the flies, sweetheart. This is the wrong country for it. I've seen too many station wives hit the bottle because they'd slipped into the habit when they were lonely and bored. It's not pretty to watch, believe me. If you want to drink, let's drink together – and if we hang one on, there's not much harm done.'

The insinuation angered her and she blazed out at him.

'What do you expect me to do? Hang around for forty-eight hours waiting for you to come home for a cocktail? If you can't trust me in a little thing like this, how can you trust me in the big ones?'

He was instantly contrite.

'Mary, I didn't mean it like that! I know this country better than you do. I understand how it can take people unaware. It's – it's like a half-tamed animal, strong, compelling, but dangerous too, if you don't handle yourself carefully. That goes for men as well as women. The territory's full of fellows who've gone native, or hit the bottle, or just simply surrendered themselves to the madness of solitude. We call 'em "hatters" – like the Mad Hatter at Alice's tea-party. At first meeting, they're normal enough, but at bottom, crazy as coots.'

His voice softened and he laid his gentle work-roughened hands on her shoulders.

'I love you, Mary. I know these first years aren't going to be easy for you. So, I try to warn you. That's all.'

The touch of him and gentleness of him charmed the anger out of her, as it always did. But this time, she could not bring herself to surrender; and, each night, at the same time, she took one drink – no more, no less – in futile affirmation of her right to be herself.

Still carrying the drink, she walked into the living-room, sat down, picked up a month-old newspaper and began leafing through it idly. The news was as dead as if it had happened on another planet, but the gossip columns and the fashion plates piqued her to jealousy of the women who lived a walk away from stores and boutiques and the daily novelties of a city. Society in the territory was limited to a clatter of voices on the pedal-radio, a picnic race-meeting and a yearly dance afterwards on one of the larger properties, where the women wore frocks that had been in mothballs for a year and the men got cheerfully drunk round the drink-table, or danced stumbling and tongue-tied to an out-of-tune piano.

It was enough, perhaps, for the others—the weathered matrons, the leggy adolescents who had never seen a city; but for her, Mary Dillon, all too little.

Memories flooded back, soft, insidious, cajoling. The drink warmed her. The paper slipped unnoticed to the floor. She dozed fitfully in the chair.

Suddenly she was awake. Big Sally was shaking her gently and the clock on the mantel read 9.45. Big Sally looked at her with questioning eyes.

'You eat now, Missus. Boss no come. Dinner all burn up finish!'

Anger took hold of her and she stood up, knocking over the glass so that it shattered on the floor. Her eyes blazed, her voice rasped hysterically.

'Put the boss's dinner in the oven. Give the rest to the girls. I'm going to bed!'

The dark woman watched her go with soft, pitying eyes, then shrugged philosophically and began to pick up the fragments of glass from the floor.

Mary Dillon hurried into the bedroom, slammed the door and threw herself on the bed, sobbing in bitterness and defeat. Lance had failed her, the country had defeated her. It was time to be quit of it all.

From his hide among the pandanus roots, Lance Dillon looked out across thirty yards of moonlit water to the myalls' camp-fires on the beach. They were squatting on their haunches, roasting a quarter of meat from the slain bull, and the smell of burnt hair drifted across the water. Each man had built a small fire at his back and the flames leapt up, highlighting the corded muscles and the sleek skin of their shoulders and breasts.

Their weapons were laid on the sand and they seemed absorbed in their meal and their talk, but at every sound – the cry of a night-bird, the leap of a fish, they became tense and watchful; their eyes searched the river and their teeth shone like new ivory out of their shadowy faces. Dillon huddled back against the wall of the bank and cautiously daubed more mud on his face, lest a chance gleam of fire or moonlight should betray his presence.

He had found this place no more than five minutes before the hunters had come stalking him down the banks, and he had been here six hours already. It was at a point where the river swung out into an elbow, with a wide beach on one side, and on the other a steep bank plunging down into deep still water. The bank was thickly grown with bush and the searching roots of the pandanus palms reached down, ten feet or more, like a fish cage into the stream, so that the drift-wood piled about them in a kind of barricade.

He was in a dangerous spot – 'croc water' the bush-men called it – but he had to choose between the certainty of a myall spear, and the chance of a big saurian, sleeping in the mud. Cautiously, he parted the driftwood and eased himself in behind the roots. His feet plunged deep into the muddy bottom and braced themselves on a buried tree-trunk. The water was waist-deep and he had to bend his shoulders painfully to find headroom under the tangled roots. But the spot was in shadow, the driftwood was thick, and on their first down-stream cast the myalls had passed within a yard of him.

When he saw their retreating backs, he had to fight against the panic temptation to break out and head for open country; but he knew that they would soon under-stand that they had missed him, and then they would come back. So he stayed, the water bleaching his skin, the leeches battening on him, a black spider dangling within an inch of his eyes, a cloud of insects buzzing frantically about him. As the cold crept into his blood, his wound began to throb painfully and he forced a thick twig between his teeth to stop their chattering.

He experimented cautiously, trying to find an easier position, but the dangers in movement were only too apparent. A piece of driftwood, dislodged and floating down-stream, an eddy of mud in the current, would betray him in a moment to the practised eyes of the pursuers. Nothing to do but wait it out and hope they gave up at nightfall.

They came back sooner than he expected. He saw them, fifty yards off, beating the banks more carefully, probing shadowy overhangs and the hollows under the bushes. One big buck was working his way swiftly towards his hiding-place. Dillon eased himself slowly down into the water until it was lapping at his chin. Then when he could see only the buttocks and knees of the pursuer, he took a deep breath and immersed himself completely in the dark water. The myall came abreast of the pile of driftwood, jerked some of it away and thrust his spear into the hollow behind. His feet churned up the muddy bottom and Dillon, an inch below the surface, held his breath until it seemed his heart must burst and the top of his head blow off. Then the myall moved away, splashing up-stream, and Dillon surfaced and gulped in great draughts of air. When he had recovered sufficiently to look about him, he saw that the screen of driftwood was breached, dangerously, and he set himself to repair it, piece by careful piece, while the myalls worked their way up-stream again, calling to each other in husky musical voices.

The ducking and the exertion dislodged the bandage and started the wound bleeding and he had to battle against the old fear of the crocodiles, while he struggled to adjust the tourniquet and the sodden dressing. Suddenly, he was desperately weary, from hunger, exertion and loss of blood and he knew that he could not stay conscious much longer. Yet, if he let himself lapse into sleep, he would slide into the water and stifle.

Painfully, he turned his head, searching in the half-light for a root or a projection that might hold him. Finding none, he undid the buckle of his belt and slid the strap out from the loops of his trouser-top. The sodden trousers sank slowly down to his ankles, but he did not care. He looped the belt high round his chest and buckled himself to one of the slim, tuberous palm roots, so that when he leaned back, his body hung, suspended under the armpits. The friction of the belt on the rough cortex might hold him while he dozed. He tested it, once, twice and again; then let his body go limp, while his mind surrendered itself to the illusion of rest.

It was no more than an illusion, pain-haunted and full of feverish terrors. Black grinning faces swelled and exploded close to his own. Bull horns gored at his ribs like spears. Mary's face, cold and withdrawn, mocked his appeal and, when his hands groped out to her, she retreated from him, hostile and pitiless. He was burning in a dark sea, drowning in a cold fire. He was swinging, a fleshless skeleton, from a twisted tree.

Then, mercifully, he woke, to moonlight and silver water, the gleam of camp-fires and the torturing smell of cooked meat. The upper part of his body was cramped and constricted, and from the waist down, there was no sensation at all. With infinite care, he began to move, easing himself out of the belt, flexing himself to reach the fallen trousers and drew them up again to his waist, biting his lips to stifle a cry as pain started in every nerve. Finally, he was standing again,

33

his feet firm on the sunken log, his back flat against the muddy bank.

A night in this place would kill him for a certainty. Before dawn, he must break out of it, find food and warmth and set the sluggish blood moving again. Soon, when the myalls had gorged themselves with meat, they would lie down like animals on the sand, and sleep till sunrise. Then, he must move; but how and where? There was the river in front and a wall of mud at his back and over all, the cold and treacherous radiance of the hunters' moon.

Mundaru, the buffalo man, was puzzled. Squatting on the sand, with fire at his belly and his back, and the meat of the totem making another warmth inside him, he thought back over each step of the trail from its beginning in the high grasses to its end in the river shallows. He timed it again; how many paces a fit man might run and walk while the shadows extended by a spear's length. He added more distance and more time to the calculation to allow for some unexpected reserve of strength in the white man – and was still convinced that he could not have out-distanced them.

Therefore, he must have left the river and struck out to open country. But at what point? Mundaru, himself, had scouted every inch of one bank and he was confident that he had missed nothing. The bucks from the other bank had sworn with equal conviction that they had overlooked nothing. But Mundaru was not so sure. This was the difference between one hunter and another, the reason for the old tribal law that the weak must share with the strong, the keen of eye must hunt for those who failed to read the signs. In the morning, he himself would cross the river and look again.

He sat a little apart from the others, a painted man, his jaws champing rhythmically on the tough meat, his eyes now scanning the water, now staring into the last leaping flames of the cook-fire. He did not speak to them, nor they to him; but their thought was clear. He was diminished in their sight by his failure to come up with the white man. They were asking themselves whether they had made a mistake by committing themselves to his leadership; whether there was not some defect in his totem relationship; whether the white man had not some malignant magic working against them and against Mundaru in particular. If their doubts persisted, they might well leave him in the morning and carry back the news of his failure to the tribe, and to Willinja, the maker of magic.

Mundaru, himself, could not go back – not without shame, not without fear of the uncompleted, ritual cycle. He must follow to the kill or to his own death, as he had when he wore the feathered boots and looked on the stone which was the secret name of a man.

Now, he had walked all round the thought and come back to the starting point. He had seen all there was to see, good and bad. He was ready for sleep. He yawned, scratched himself, and stretched his body on the sand, working a hollow for himself between the two fires. Then he drew his spears to within a hand's reach and, without a word to his companions, closed his eyes. But sleep would not come. His thoughts flew back, like a green parrot, to the camp, where Menyan would be sleeping by the side of her husband, Willinja, the sorcerer.

She was named for the moon, the new moon, slim and young. When she was still a child, her father had promised her to Willinja, because he needed the favour of a man who understood the secrets of the dream-people, who could make rain and call death into the body of an enemy. From the moment of this promise, she was wedded to Willinja. She slept at his fire. His women taught her. She learned all that a wife should know to be valuable to her husband. But he did not take her until she had become a woman and had sat in the secret place, covered with leaves and eating none but the foods permitted to a woman at the time of blood.

From this moment, she was lost to Mundaru. But he still desired her. He sought occasions to meet her alone, to speak with her, out of sight of the other women. He was young, while her husband was old. He was pleasing to her. Her eyes told him that; but she was afraid of her husband – as Mundaru was afraid. Because Willinja's cold eyes could look into the marrow of a man's brain and his spirit travelled abroad out of his body, seeing what was done in the most secret places.

Even now, on the edge of sleep, Mundaru could feel his hostile presence, shepherding his thoughts away from Menyan. He must not fight him – yet. But with the white man dead, and the white man's strength absorbed into himself, then, he might be ready to enter into open conflict. A small, cold tremor of anticipation shook him, then burrowing deeper into the warmth of the sand, he composed himself for sleep.

The bucks watched him, with sidelong speculative eyes. They talked a little in low voices, then they too stretched themselves on the sand and before the flames had died to a dull red glow, they were snoring like tired animals.

To Lance Dillon, penned in the small, liquid darkness under the pandanus roots, had come a small ray of hope. It was a moonbeam, slanting down from a point above his head and falling on the black, still water in front of him. Inch by inch, he slewed himself round in the confined space until, looking up, he could see a narrow opening between the upper roots and the mud bank. It was, perhaps, three feet above his head, and he judged it almost large enough to take his head and shoulders. If he could reach it and pass through it, he might scale the high bank under the shadows of the bushes and head across the grass flats away from the sleeping myalls.

It was a big 'if'. He was very weak. One arm and shoulder were useless and this gymnastic effort might well prove too much for him. The slightest noise would brings the myalls leaping to their feet and splashing across the river. The first problem was the bank itself.

The black soil was damp and slippery and its contours were clotted into large projections, any one of which might break away and fall noisily into the water.

With infinite care, he began to scoop out with his hands, a foothold just above the water-line. As each handful was dug, he laid it gently in the water, letting it float soundlessly away from his palm. He dug deep, so that his feet would not slide, he groped around the mouth of the hole, feeling for friable pieces that might fall away under pressure. Then, when the two lower holes were dug, he reached up and hollowed two more above his head.

It was a child's labour, but before it was done, he was trembling as if in ague and the sweat was running down his face. Then, new risks presented themselves. His clothing was full of water. The moment he climbed upwards, it would spill out, noisily, into the pool. The roots above his head were matted and rough. They might tangle themselves in his belt or in the loose, flapping fabric.

Bracing himself against one of the log roots, he bent down into the water and took off his boots. The simple operation took a long time. The laces were leather, tight-drawn and slippery. He had to rest many times before he was free of them. Trousers and shirt came next, and, as he worked his way out of them, he could feel the leeches, squamous and bloated, clinging to his flesh. He tried to pull them off, but they clung all the tighter. He must endure them a while longer while they drained him of blood he could ill afford to lose. He crouched mother-naked in the pool, debating whether to try to salvage his clothing against the heat of the coming day. Finally, he decided against it and let the sodden garments sink to the bottom of the pool.

He was ready now – ready to make the attempt on which his life depended. He looked up towards the narrow opening where the moonlight gleamed, then, with a wracking effort, hoisted himself into the first foothold. Behind him, in the water, floated the spearhead and the broken haft which had slipped, unnoticed, from his grasp while he was preparing himself for sleep.

CHAPTER THREE

FOR SERGEANT NEIL ADAMS, Northern Territory Mounted Police, the dog days were coming. He knew the symptoms: the day-long depression, the restless nights, the itch in the blood for whisky or a woman or an honest-to-God brawl – anything to break the crushing monotony of life in the outback emptiness. The disease itself was endemic and recurrent – regular as the lunar periods. It had a name in all languages: *Weltschmerz, cafard*, and, here in the territory, they called it simply 'gone troppo'.

It began as a languor, a distaste for the repetitive elements of living: food, work, company and confinement. It built to a brooding moroseness, which lasted sometimes for days, sometimes for weeks, and in chronic cases, became permanent.

Its climax was a feverish melancholy which broke usually in a catharsis of violence or drunkenness but ended, sometimes, in suicide or murder.

No one who lived long in the Territory escaped it utterly. All, in one fashion or another, were marked by it, as folks are marked by the yellow tinge of latent malaria. The 'hatters' surrendered themselves to solitude and crazy contemplations. The cattlemen and the drovers hit the outback settlements and launched themselves into a week of drinking and fighting. The stock-

boys and the station aborigines grew sullen and dis-
obedient and finally went walkabout into the bush.
Women became tearful and shrewish. Some of them
lasped into brief heart-breaking love affairs with the
nearest available man; so that one more item of gossip
was bruited in the bars from Darwin to Alice Springs,
from Broome to Mataranka. Only the intelligent, the
disciplined, the responsible managed to suppress it, as
malaria is suppressed, by therapeutic treatment.

For Sergeant Neil Adams, the treatment was simple
– work, and more work.

His headquarters were at Ochre Bluffs, a small
huddle of clap-board buildings under the lee of a range
of red hills. His territory extended a hundred miles in
every direction and included a mixed population of
cattlemen, publicans, storekeepers, two doctors, four
bush nurses, transient pilots, stock inspectors, well-
sinkers, drifters and whites 'gone native'. His duties
were legion. He took the census, sobered drunks,
tracked down tribal killers, settled disputes on brands
and boundaries, registered births, marriages and deaths,
leprosy and syphilis.

Much of it was paper-work in the dusty office of his
bungalow at Ochre Bluffs. The rest of it meant days
in the saddle, nights by a camp-fire, with Billy-Jo, the
aboriginal tracker, for company. Yet in the sprawling,
inchoate life of the territory, he was a symbol of
security, of ultimate order. He could not afford to be
a drunk or a lecher or a chaser of tribal women. At
the first lapse, his authority would be destroyed completely.

41

So, when the black mood began to grow on him, he would saddle and ride away from Ochre Bluffs, into the myall country. Billy-Jo would pick up the tracks of a nomad group, and follow them – for days sometimes – to a water-hole or a river-bed. He would talk with the elders, look to the sick, note the new-born and the dead, pick up hints of feuds and medicine killings. At night, he would sit by their fires, listening to their songs, watching the dances of the men, piecing out, step by step, the intimate progression of their lives, adding a new word or a new symbol to his knowledge. Practice had made him proficient in the exercise, and after a while, his old identity would fall away; he would find himself absorbed in an ancient, complex life, from which he would emerge relaxed, renewed and ready for a new effort.

He had one inflexible rule. At such times, he never went near a homestead unless called to an emergency. He was thirty-five years of age, six feet tall, handsome in a rugged fashion and full of the sap of manhood. He knew himself too well to trust himself to the company of a lonely woman whose husband might be absent for days at a time. He had learnt his lesson early, at the cost of one near-tragedy. He liked his job. He had the taste for dependence and authority. He knew the price he had to pay to keep them. For the rest, there was a month's leave every year; and what he did with it was his own affair.

So, a few minutes before nine on this raw, hot morning, he sat in his office, smoking the first cigarette of the day and waiting for the radio circuit to open. Soon, the monitor station at Jamieson's Creek would come on the air, calling in, one by one, the homesteads and the mission stations and the police offices over three thousand square miles of territory. They would report their needs and their problems. They would pin-point the locations of the flying doctor and the bush nurses and the mail-plane. Adams would detail his own movements and tell where he could be found on each day of his trip. Telegrams would be passed; news and gossip exchanged. When it was over, he would be free to go and purge his own devils in the privacy of the emptiest continent on the planet.

He walked across to the set, switched on and waited. Dead on the hour, the voice of the monitor came crackling in:

'LXR . . . Jamieson's Creek calling in Network One. Check in everybody, please. . . . LXR, Jamieson's Creek. . . . Nine o'clock call-in. No traffic until everyone has reported. Come in, Coolangi . . .'

And then roll-call began.

'This is Coolangi. We're in.'

'This is Boolala . . .'

'Hilda Springs in and waiting . . .'

Behind each distorted voice was a face, a family, a community, and Neil Adams knew them all. Knew them by name and habit, by bank-roll and taste in liquor. They were, in a very real sense, his people. The monitor went on calling steadily through the check-list and each station answered briskly and briefly. But when he called Minardoo homestead, there was a change. A woman's voice, high and urgent, answered.

'Hold it, please! Hold it! This is an emergency. I'm Mary Dillon.'

The monitor reassured her, calmly.

'O.K., Mrs Dillon. We've got you. Let's have it slow and clear. What's the trouble?'

Neil Adams turned up his amplifier and listened attentively. Mary Dillon's voice filled his small room.

'It's my husband. He was due home last night. He didn't come. The stockboys found his horse wandering near the homestead this morning. There was blood on the saddle. I've sent them out to look for him, but I'm worried, dreadfully worried.'

Fifty listeners heard her, and felt for her, but only the monitor answered.

'Hold it, Mrs Dillon. . . . Did you get that, Sergeant Adams?'

'Adams here. I've got it. Let me talk please. Mrs Dillon, can you hear me?'

'I hear you, yes.'

'I want you to answer my questions clearly and simply. First, where did your husband go yesterday?'

'He went to a breeding pen we've got, just behind red ridge. Twenty miles more or less from the homestead.'

'Anyone go with him?'

'No. All the stockmen were out mustering.'

'When the pony came in, was he lathered?'

'No. Jimmy, the head stockman, said he must have just ambled home during the night. He was reasonably fresh.'

'Has anyone gone out to look for your husband?'

44

'Yes. Jimmy and four boys.'

'What did Jimmy say about the blood on the saddle?'

'He – he said he didn't like it. But he wouldn't add anything.'

'All right, Mrs Dillon, just sit tight a moment. I'll talk to you again. . . . Does anybody know if there's a plane near Ochre Bluffs? Over.'

Out of the crackle of static, a new voice answered, a thick Scots burr with an edge of humour under it.

'This is Jock Campbell, laddie. Gilligan's due in with the mail in twenty minutes. He's flying the Auster. Do you want me to send him over for you?'

'Yes, please, Jock. Tell him two passengers with packs. Me and Billy-Jo.'

'Will do, laddie. I'll tell him the score. Expect him in about an hour and a half. Over.'

'Mrs Dillon? Sergeant Adams again. I'm coming over with Tommy Gilligan. With luck I'll be there in three hours. I'm bringing a tracker. I want two saddle-horses and pack-pony. Also, make me up a medical kit. Bandages, antiseptic, sulpha-powder and whisky. Is that clear?'

'Quite clear. I'll be waiting.'

'Jamieson Creek? Pass the word to the doctor. Keep a check on his movements. I may have to get in touch with him in a hurry. Is there anything more for me?'

'No. . . . All clear, Neil. We'll hold the routine stuff. If anything urgent crops up, we'll know where to get you. Good luck. Good luck, Mrs Dillon, and we'll be waiting for news. Don't worry too much. Over to you, Neil.'

'Thanks, man. Ochre Bluffs, over and out.'

Neil Adams flipped off the power and began to pace thoughtfully up and down the narrow office.

Mary Dillon's report troubled him – for more reasons than one. At first blush, it was a commonplace bush accident: a man thrown from his horse and sweating it out with a broken arm or leg until the stockboys came to find him. Some survived it, some didn't. But, normally, the policeman simply took the reports and waited until the station staff had made their own search; by which time it was a case either for a doctor or an undertaker. But blood on a man's saddle meant trouble – blackfellow trouble: and this was always police business.

Tribal violence against the white had died out long ago. Single incidents were now so rare as to be sensational; and they were generally connected with women, smuggled liquor or the intrusion of shady characters into tribal preserves. But, whatever their cause, they were a headache to the local police authority. Native affairs were a tender political issue in the Federal Capital as in the Territory itself. The Government needed to make a good showing in United Nations, to bolster its Trusteeship claims in New Guinea. It fostered education, social betterment, ultimate integration. The cattle interests were less enthusiastic. They depended on aboriginal and half-caste labour to run their holdings cheaply. They were committed to the *status quo* – and they opposed anything that looked like

46

soft handling of the natives. The unwary policeman was apt to find himself caught between the upper and the nether millstones.

All this was only part of Adams's problem. The other half it was Mary Dillon herself.

Of all the women in his territory, this was the one to whom he felt himself the most vulnerable. He had seen her first at a dance on Coolangi Station, a slim, dark woman in a modish bouffant frock, strangely out of place among the local matrons and their suntanned daughters. He remembered the smile she gave him when he asked her to dance, the feel of her body as she relaxed in his arms, her relief when he was able to talk about things that interested her, the hint of fear and discontent when she talked of her own life in the Territory. He understood how she felt. Lance Dillon was a man ploughing a rough furrow, a driving, persistent man, with little understanding of women. He had neither the time nor the wit to give this one what she needed.

But Neil Adams understood. Neil Adams had time, passion and a practised bachelor's way with the ladies. While Dillon was swapping stories at the bar, he squired Mary through the introductions, charmed her with tales of his roving life and made her laugh with the spicier gossip of the outback.

They had warmed to each other, but a mutual caution had made them withdraw from intimacy of voice or gesture. When the evening was over, she had thanked him without coquetry and let him hand her back to her husband. Three or four times since then, he had met her at the homestead with Dillon and they had welcomed him with the offhand friendliness of the bush. But the memory of that first night still clung to him: the sound of her voice, the heady drift of her perfume, an itch in his blood when the dark moods took him.

Now, they must meet again, alone with the unspoken attraction between them and her husband hurt or dead on the fringe of the Stone Country.

He frowned and ran his fingers through his hair in a gesture of impatience and indecision; then he walked to the door and shouted for Billy-Jo, the black tracker.

Willinja, the sorcerer, sat in the shadow of a high rock and waited for the men of the tribe to come to him.

The rocks was shaped like Willinja's own totem, the Kangaroo – broad base, which was the rump of the animal, tapering upwards to a small head, on which two projections stood up like the pricked ears of the marsupial. When the sun was climbing, as it was now, the shadow fell upon Willinja, and the small head lay forward of him, the ears pressed to the dust, listening.

Behind the rock, in the full blaze of sun, was a waterhole which, even in the drought time, never quite dried up. There were thus the sun, the water-hole, the rock, the man, and the shadow covering the man and extending beyond him. Their positions, their relationship to one another had ritual significance.

The pool took knowledge from the sun, which saw

everything. The rock drank knowledge from the pool, but sheltered the sorcerer from the malignant reflection of his own magic. Through the shadow, it passed on power and protection, and the listening ears searched out secrets even in the dust.

Willinja himself sat cross-legged on the ground, his face turned towards the encampment from which the men would come to him. In the dry dust, he had drawn, with a sharpened stick, the totems of the tribe: the great snake, the buffalo, the crocodile and the fish which is called barramundi. Each drawing showed the outline of the animal, and the framework of bones inside it, as if an all-seeing eye had stripped off the meat and muscle to come to the core of the being.

Behind the drawings were laid out the instruments of Willinja's magic: a round river stone, marked with ochre; a long sliver of quartzite pointed at one end, and at the other, coated with gum and trailing long strands of human hair; a small bark dilly-bag containing human bones.

The sorcerer was a tall man, strong but ageing, so that the skin of his body puckered and wrinkled over the long decorative scars on his chest and belly. His mouth was wide and full of yellow teeth. His broad, flat nose receded into the craggy brows, from which quick eyes stared out across the sunlit plain. His hair and his beard were grey, but powdered with ochre dust, so that against the dark skin of his face, they stood out like fire.

To the ignorant and to the stranger, Willinja was a nothing – a primitive squatting in the dust, toying with

49

childish trifles. To his own people, he was a man of power, a keeper of ancient knowledge, an initiate of the spirit-folk who, at the time of his induction, had killed him, dismembered him and then made him whole again, gluing his parts together with magical substances. When personal or tribal life was disturbed by malignant influences, he alone had the formulas and the power to use them for the restoration of order and well-being. He was not a charlatan. He believed in himself. The spirits had made him what he was and their potency worked in him and through him.

Now the men were coming towards him from the direction of the camp. They came in three groups, the first carrying spears and clubs, the second, bearing sticks and the long, deep-voiced instrument of music which is called the didjeridoo. Behind them, unarmed, lagging and shame-faced, walked the men of the buffalo totem who had been Mundaru's companions at the killing and who, two hours after sunrise, had returned to the tribe without him.

Questioned by Willinja and the elders, they had told of the killing of the bull, the wounding of the white man and Mundaru's pursuit of him. They did not think to lie. They knew that Willinja saw the truth with spirit eyes. On this level they were afraid of him. On the lower one, they understood his jealousy of Mundaru and hoped to make it work in their favour.

Willinja watched them through narrowed eyes, feeling the power rise in him, collecting himself for the ritual which must follow.

When the first group came they settled themselves

in two files, facing each other to the right and the left of Willinja, the musicians on one side, the spearmen on the other. When the buffalo men arrived, they sat in a line facing Willinja so that between them all was a hollow square of sacred ground. There were no women, no children. They had gone off in the opposite direction, gathering food; for to look on what was done in the secret place meant terrible and sudden death.

They were seated now, and waiting. Willinja closed his eyes and sat rock-rigid under the mantling shadow. He could feel all his vitality being sucked upward and concentrated inside his skull-case. After a long while, he began to speak in the spirit voice, which issued more like a chant than normal speech.

'There is earth and there is water. The wind blows over the earth, but does not shake it. The leaf floats on the river, but does not harm it. We are the river and the earth. The white man is the leaf and the wind. . . .'

The buffalo men sat silent, but the spearmen and the music-men gave a long-drawn cry of approval. . . .

'Ai – eee – ah !'

'We have lived in peace. We have slept safe with full bellies. Our spirit places are untouched because the white man and his people pass by like wind and the blown leaf.'

His voice rose to a high, wailing pitch.

'Until now . . . ! Until Mundaru and his friends raise the anger of the spirit people – so that the wind is now an angry voice and the leaf grows into a tree and the tree becomes a club and a spear to destroy us.'

'Ai – eee!' cried the spearmen. And the music-men cried louder. . . .

'Ai ee – ah!'

Willinja leaned forward, pointing at the drawing of the buffalo in the dust.

'This is Anaburu, the buffalo, which is the sign of Mundaru. This he may kill and eat, and no one would refuse him. But this . . .'

He scrawled swiftly in the dust a new outline representing the big Brahman bull.

'This is not Anaburu. This is another thing, a white man's animal. There is no life in it for Mundaru. But he kills it – and now he tries to kill the white man. If he does that, there is death for all of us. The other white men will come and move us away, to a strange country, where our spirits will forget us and we will wither and die. We will be the wind. We will be the leaf, lost and drifting nowhere. Where then shall we put our dead? Who will sing them into peace? This has happened before. Now it can happen to us, the men of Gimbi.'

He broke off. The buffalo men sat, bowed in guilt; but this time there was no answering chant from the others. They held themselves erect and silent, touched with fear at this imminent threat of expatriation – of exile from the earth which was their only source of life and tribal identity.

Willinja watched them, and knew that he held them in the hollow of his hand. He waited, so that they might suffer their fear a little longer. Then he dropped his voice to a low, soft key.

'I have talked with the spirit men. I have heard their voices answering. They say there is a hope for us, if the death that threatens us is sung into the body of Mundaru!'

Immediately, the fear went out of them, in a long, audible exhalation. There was no protest, only relief. The victim had been named. With the spilling of his blood, the land and the tribe would settle back to peace and security.

Willinja, the sorcerer, stood up. From the row of objects in front of him, he picked up the stone with its ochre markings and laid it in the centre of the square where all could see it. They knew what it was – the symbol of a man, whose name was Mundaru. What was sung into the stone would be sung into the man. He could no more move to escape it than the stone could walk away across the dust.

Willinja walked back to his place, knelt on one knee and picked up the long, quartzite blade, with its haft of gum and its trailing pennon of hair. Then he flung out his arm and pointed it, straight at the stone which bore the name of Mundaru. The others watched, tense and silent. The blade was a spirit spear, pointed at the victim. The gum was fuel to burn his entrails. The hair would make it fly straight and true towards its target.

Then, abruptly, the singing began – a low heavily-accented chant, its rhythm beaten out on the hollow sticks, its melody counter-pointed by the deep, throbbing notes of the didjeridoo. Every line of it was a death wish, directed against the man-stone in the dust.

'May the spear strike straight to his heart. . . .'

'May the fire burn his entrails. . . .'

'May the Great Serpent eat his liver. . . .'

On and on it went, a projective sorcery directed against an absent man, an accumulation of malignities, sung over and over again while the sun climbed in the sky and the shadow of the kangaroo rock grew shorter and shorter, until it reached the feet of Willinja.

When it did so, the chanting stopped. Willinja put down the spirit spear, and with a gesture of finality, obliterated the drawings he had made in the dust. The spearmen and the musicians stood up, walked slowly round the death stone, then, by common accord, headed back to the camp. Only the buffalo men remained. They had been partners in crime. Now they must be the instruments of punishment.

They waited, submissive and patient until Willinja showed them how and when and with what sacred ritual they must kill Mundaru.

Naked as Adam in his primal Eden, Lance Dillon lay on a patch of warm mud and looked up at the sky through a meshwork of reeds and swamp-grass. He had slept a long time, and he was still lapped in the languor of rest and warmth and ebbing fever. He felt no pain, no fear, only the genial detachment of a ghost sitting on a fence and looking down on its own discarded body.

It wasn't much of a body any more – a poor caricature of Lance Dillon, the land-tamer. It was streaked all over with mud, from the midnight climb up the river-bank, scored into weals by brambles and thorn-bushes and the bites of swamp insects. One shoulder was a pulpy red mass, from which the tracks of infection spread out like ganglia. Leeches clung to it, gnats swarmed about it, ants tracked over it with impunity. Its mouth was twisted in a rictus of unfelt pain, its eyes, inflamed and bloodshot, stared up at the morning sky. But it still belonged to him. Life was still pulsing sluggishly under the welted skin, and somewhere, inside his skull, pain and panic and hunger-pangs were beginning to wake again. However unwillingly, the ghost must step down from the fence and enter again into his battered habitation.

But not yet, not just yet. This small suspension of pain was too precious to surrender. He must use it to take hold of reason before it slipped away for ever.

He had left the river. He remembered that. He had climbed the bank from the dark pool to the bright moonlight, while the myalls slept by the embers of their fires. He had lain a long time under a bramble-bush, husbanding his strength and trying to plot himself a course across the grass country. Beyond the bush was swamp-grass, and beyond the grass, a billabong – a long, narrow lagoon, fringed with reeds, covered with lily-pads, whose bulbous roots would give him food.

Again, his problem was to reach it without leaving tracks. When he crawled out from the bush across a small, clear patch, towards the grasses, he dragged after him a small, dead branch, like a broom, to sweep away

55

the marks of hands and knees. When morning came, there would be dew on the ground, and, with luck, the myall trackers might miss him. Reaching the fringe of grass, he parted the tall stems carefully and stepped over them so that they swung back, an unbroken wall of greenery. He heaved the thorn branch away and began to crawl towards the swamp.

He reached it sooner than he expected and, anchoring himself to a small reed-covered bank, began to scrabble for the roots under the broad lily leaves and the sleeping flowers. They were watery and bitter, and at the first mouthfuls, he retched, painfully. But, after a time, he managed to hold some down; then he lay down on the wet mud, and, in spite of the insects and the swamp noises, slept till the sun was high.

Now the sleep was over, the last drugged languor gone. He was no longer free, but burdened with a body, cramped in every muscle, bitten on every inch of skin, with poison spreading out from the festering wound in his shoulder. Painfully, he worked himself to a sitting position and scooped up mouthfuls of the still, swamp water. He crammed a lily root into his mouth and chewed on it slowly until he was able to swallow.

Before him, the water lay bright in the sun. The lily-flowers were open. The green slime in the shallows shone with a sickly brilliance, and the ripples spread out from a brood of cruising ducklings. Against the farther reeds, a pair of egrets stood, contemplating the flat water and waiting for an unwary fish. The lagoon was full of life and full of food; but he was too weak to hunt it, and he dared not raise his head above the high grasses, for fear the myalls might be watching.

This was his chief terror now; that he could not surrender himself to the simplest instinctive gesture. He must think with two minds – the mind of the hunter and that of the fugitive. Every move must be planned and measured to his small strength. He could not think of combat – only of flight and concealment. This discipline of terror made him shut out of his mind every other thought – of Mary, of the homestead, even of ultimate rescue. He could count on nothing and nobody but himself.

Suddenly, out of the blank sky, he heard the aircraft . . .

Mundaru, the buffalo man, heard it too. He leaned on his spear and looked up, searching the air for the big bird which carried the white men in its belly; but the bird was flying in the track of the sun and for a long while he could not see it. Of the bird itself, he had no fear. He had seen it many times, and wondered at the magic which could command such a messenger. But the men inside it were another matter. These he had good reason to fear.

Earlier in the morning, before his companions had left him, they had warned him of just such a coming. There was a power the white men had to call each other over great distances and, when they called, the big bird always came, sometimes with the policeman,

Adamidji, sometimes with the other, who carried a powerful magic in a little black bag. For this reason, they would not stay with Mundaru any longer. They would go back to the camp and – they did not say this, though Mundaru understood it very well – they would seek counsel and protection from the evil that had already been done.

Mundaru had not argued. He had shrugged and let them go. He had expected no better. Once a man stepped outside the tribal framework, he was naked and alone, with only his totem to help. But he was still afraid of the displeasure of the tribe and of the potent magic of Willinja.

But he was committed and he could not turn back. When the others had gone he set himself to search every inch of the farther bank, along the water and the high ground above. So far, he had found nothing. The dew was still fresh in the sheltered places; in the open, the ground was crusted and brittle. There was no depression in the grasses, where a wounded man might have lain. The only thing that puzzled him was a thorn-branch, dried and broken, lying fifty paces from its parent-tree.

The big bird was closer now. He heard its pulsing roar filling the air. Then, as it dived out of the sun-track, he saw it, banking in a high, wide turn over the swamp-lands.

As he followed it, his eye was caught by a movement faraway near the edge of the lagoon. The movement was repeated, and when he turned to it, he saw, diminished by the distance, the head and shoulders of a man and one arm waving frantically at the droning bird.

Mundaru stood, stock still, waiting to see what the bird would do. It swung round slowly, completing its turn and headed away towards the homestead. The head and the waving arm disappeared, but a gaggle of geese and swamp duck was rising and clattering above the lagoon. Before the last sound of the plane had died out of the sky, Mundaru stooped and, silent as a snake, began thrusting through the waving grasses towards the lily-pond.

CHAPTER FOUR

IT IS ONE of the ironies of existence that a man's life
may hang on the humour of his surgeon's wife, or the
state of a taxi-driver's liver, or the angle of sight from
a bucketing aircraft. At the precise moment when
Adams might have seen Dillon waving from the grass,
his attention was caught by Billy-Jo, shouting in his
ear and pointing out through the perspex window.

'Look, boss! Kirrkie come up! Bird belong dead
thing.'

Sighting along the black-tracker's hand, Adams saw,
high above a sandstone saddle, the wheeling flight of
hundreds of kite-hawks, sure sign to the bushman of
a carrion kill. He leaned forward, tapped Gilligan, the
pilot, on the shoulder and shouted in his ear.

'Over to the right – behind the ridges!'

Gilligan gave him the thumbs-up sign, banked and
headed for the red hills. As the aircraft came in, low
and lurching through the air, the kites rose, screaming, and Adams looked down to see the green valley,
the brood cows cropping contentedly with their calves
at heel, and, in the centre, the mangled carcase on
which the kites had been feeding.

The next moment he was flung violently back in his
seat, as the plane climbed steeply to clear the saddle.
When he levelled off, Adams tapped him again.

'Any chance of putting her down in there?'

Gilligan shook his head and shouted:

'Not a hope. It looks flat enough because of the grass, but we'd probably tear the undercart off!'

'Can you make another circuit?'

'Sure!'

As he banked and turned again, Billy-Jo turned to Adams.

'Boss! I know this place! Spirit caves for Gimbi tribe!'

'You sure of that, Billy-Jo?'

'Sure, boss! White man's cows in spirit-place. Maybe Gimbi men make trouble, eh?'

Adams nodded thoughtfully, staring out at the red scoriated rocks and the rich pastures between them. It was, at least, a working hypothesis. Half the trouble in the territory began with the clash between the pragmatic philosophy of the whites and the dream-time thinking of the aborigines. The small aircraft rocked again as Gilligan lifted it over the ridge. Gilligan turned back and shouted:

'Where to now?'

'Head for the homestead. See what we can pick up on the way.'

'Roger!'

The Auster lurched and shuddered in the air-currents that rose from the hot earth, and Adams sweated and battled against the nausea that threatened him at every moment. Billy-Jo called to him again:

'Stockboys, boss!'

They were riding in line abreast, strung out across

half a mile of grassland and sparse timber. When they saw the aircraft they reined in and waved their hats in greeting. Adams counted them – five in all. They would be the riders from Minardoo, and they had still not found Lance Dillon. Again he questioned Gilligan.

'I'd like to talk to 'em. Any hope at all of a landing?'

'Look for yourself! Rocks and ant-hills! I daren't risk it – unless you want to walk home. . . .'

Adams grinned and shook his head.

'No, thanks. Cruise around for a bit. Let's see if we can spot any myalls.'

He was not sure what he was looking for; he was simply going through a routine – assembling the sparse human elements in this big country, setting them in their geographic location, in the hope that the geographic relationship might develop into a human one. A man, black or white, was in a given place for a specific reason. His reason and his attitudes were, normally, predictable. There was no place for strollers and vagabonds in the outback. The country was too harsh, the loneliness too oppressive, to coax them outside the familiar circuits of water-hole and game-land and grazing areas and sacred places.

In the next fifteen minutes, he saw nothing that deviated from a work-a-day pattern of primitive life: a dozen women, waist-deep in a lily-pond, another group digging for yams on a river flat, three bucks flushing an old-man kangaroo out of the paper-bark trees, a lone man squatting in the lee of a conical rock, a deserted camp, with lean-to shelters made of bark, and thin smoke rising from the sand-covered fires.

The things he needed to see were hidden from him: Lance Dillon crouching in the swamp-reed, Mundaru, working his way through the six-foot grasses, the buffalo men in a limestone cave, burning their small toes with a hot stone, then dislocating them, and, afterwards, putting on the feathered kadaitja boots which are always worn in a ritual killing.

Adams leaned forward and tapped Gilligan on the shoulder.

'That's the best we can do from up here. Make for the homestead.'

Five minutes later they were bumping across the runway to where Mary Dillon was waiting for them.

She came to him, running, a slim, dark woman in a mannish shirt and jodhpurs, her face flushed from the sun, her hair wind-blown from the slipstream of the aircraft. At the last step she stumbled, and almost fell into his arms. He held her for a moment longer than was necessary, feeling her need and her relief and her unconscious clinging to him. Then, reluctantly, he released her. With Gilligan and Billy-Jo looking on, his greeting was studiously formal.

'Hope you haven't been too worried, Mrs Dillon. We made a circuit of the property before we came in.'

'Did you see anything?'

The eagerness in her voice gave him an odd pang of regret. He shook his head.

'Only your stockmen. They haven't found anything yet.'

Her face crumpled into fear and disappointment.

'We flew over the valley behind the sandstone bluffs. That's where your husband was going, wasn't it?'

'Yes. That's where the breeding herd was. You didn't see him there?'

'No. . . . But one of the animals was dead. It looked like the bull.'

'Oh no!'

The terror in her voice seemed disproportionate to the occasion. Adams questioned her gently.

'Is it so important, Mrs Dillon?'

Her voice rose on a high, hysterical note.

'Important! Everything we had was there! We paid three thousand pounds for that bull. Mortgaged ourselves to the neck to buy it. Lance said it was our only hope of holding out and making a success.

'I'm sorry.' What else was there to say? He shot a quick glance at Billy-Jo. The black-tracker's eyes flickered in agreement with his unspoken thought. Dillon would not kill his own animal. If the myalls had done it and he had come upon them in the act . . .

Mary's voice challenged him sharply.

'What does it mean, Neil?'

'We don't know yet, Mary; and there's no point in making nightmares for ourselves. As soon as we're ready, we'll ride out and see. Can you give us a quick lunch? It's a half-day ride.'

'Of course. It's ready for you now. The horses are saddled and the packs are made up.'

'Good girl!' He turned to the pilot. 'You'd better eat with us, Gilligan. I'll want you to look out for a few things on the way back.'

64

'Suits me, Neil. I'm hungry, anyway.'

'Let's go, Mary.'

They turned and walked towards the homestead, with Gilligan and the black-tracker walking behind them.

Luncheon was a hurried meal and a dismal one. Mary Dillon was full of questions which Adams parried carefully, because he did not want to be drawn into speculation on the fate of her husband. Gilligan's attempts to brighten the conversation with territory gossip fell flat, and after a while they ate in silence. When they had finished, Adams sent Mary outside to check the supplies on the pack-ponies, while he had a swift, private conference with the pilot.

'This looks bad, Gilligan.'

The pilot nodded.

'Time's running against us. We've got a twenty-mile ride before we even reach the Stone Country. Dillon could be dead already.'

'What do you want me to do, Neil?'

'Can you make another flight out this way tomorrow morning?'

'If it's a police matter, sure.'

'How much runway do you need to land?'

'Three hundred yards'll do me. Provided it's clear.'

'I'll try to find you one. When we catch up with the stockboys, I'll set them clearing a strip. Billy-Jo and I will try to pick up Dillon's tracks. Better we don't have a whole mob milling about and messing up the signs.'

'How will I know where you are?'

'We'll build a smoke fire. If we want you to land, we'll lay the word in stones on the ground.'

'If not?'

'Make the same flight the following day. After that, I don't think it will matter.'

'Blackfellow trouble?'

'I think so.'

Gilligan whistled softly and jerked a significant thumb towards the door.

'Are you going to tell her?'

Adams frowned and shook his head.

'Not before I have to. When you get back, pass the word round, but keep it general. I'm not sure of anything myself yet.'

'Will do, Neil. And good luck.'

They shook hands and walked out into the sunlight, where Mary was fixing the last straps on the saddlebags and Billy-Jo was examining the shoe-prints of Lance Dillon's pony. Gilligan made his farewells to Mary and Adams went with him to watch the take-off. When he came back, he saw for the first time that there were three saddle-horses instead of two, and that the pack-ponies also carried blanket-rolls and ground-sheets and water-bags for three. Before he had time to comment, Mary told him in a rush of words.

'I'm coming with you, Neil. Lance is my husband and – and I think I'd go mad if I had to wait here for news.'

For a moment, he was tempted to refuse violently. All his experience – of the country, of women, and of himself – told him that this was a dangerous folly. Instead, he grinned and said simply:

'Better bring something warm. The nights are damned chill. Pack some liniment too – you'll have saddle sores before you're much older.'

'Thank you, Neil.'

She gave him a small, grateful smile and hurried inside. Neil Adams shrugged and began to check the saddle-girths and the set of the packs, while his private devils grinned sardonically at so easy a surrender.

Lance Dillon was very near to despair. The moment he had leapt up from his hiding-place and tried to signal the aircraft, he knew that he had made a fatal mistake. Even had the pilot seen him, he would have understood little of his situation, and even had he understood, there was little he could have done about it. The nearest safe landing-strip was at the homestead, twenty miles away, and no pilot on earth would have attempted a landing in the swamp-lands. In one futile gesture he had expended his strength, and the advantage he had gained during the night.

Now, for a certainty, his pursuers would be on his track. He had not seen them, but he had no doubt at all that they had seen him. Soon, very soon, they would come to beat him out of his hiding-place. He was trapped between the grass and the lily-water, a pale frog on a mud-patch waiting for the urchins to scoop him up in a bottle.

A sob of weariness shook him, and the first tears since childhood forced themselves from his eyes. Self-pity swamped him and every instinct urged him to lie down and wait for the merciful release of a spear thrust. He buried his face in his muddy arms and wept like a baby.

After a while, the weeping calmed him, and he began to take note of the swamp noises: the shrilling of the cicadas, the low buzz of the insects, the susurration of the grass, the occasional boom of a frog, and the chitter of a pecking reed-hen. There was a rhythm to it, he found, a comforting regularity, as if the giant land were snoring and wheezing in its noonday doze.

Suddenly, the rhythm was broken. Far away to his left, there was a shrill squawking, and a few seconds later a big jabiru flapped its ungainly way over his head. He knew what it meant, and the knowledge jerked him back to reality. The hunters had flushed the bird as, soon, they must flush the man. Desperately, he tried to discipline his thoughts. There was no way of escape, and there was no weapon to his hand, but the swaying reeds.

'The reeds . . . !'

From somewhere out of a forgotten story-book, a picture presented itself, vivid as a vision: a prisoner, hunted by his gaolers, hiding in a stream and breathing through a reed. His reaction was immediate. He grasped a handful of reeds and tried to tear them out, but the tough fibres resisted him and the stalks frayed in his hands. A few second of reasoning showed him a simpler way. He knelt and bit off a pair of stalks close to the root. Then he bit off the tops, tested them by suction, and found that the air flowed freely.

With infinite care, he slid himself into the water, feet first, at a spot where the green scum had parted. When he found it deep enough, he exhaled, so that his body sank to the bottom, and then, anchoring himself to the mud, he worked his way slowly under the lily roots, feeling blindly for a snag or a sunken tree that might hold his buoyant body submerged. His rib-cage was almost bursting before he found it, but he hooked his toes under it and let his body lie diagonally under the surface, face upward, so that the reed projected upward through the lily pads. He had to blow desperately to clear it of mud and scum, but finally he was able to breathe in short, regular gasps through his mouth.

His body tended to drift upward against the anchoring feet, and the stretch of his muscles was a painful strain, but after a few moments, he began to hold himself in equilibrium, breathing the while through the slim reed. He could see nothing but the dull underside of the lily-pads, and the vague bulbous shapes of their roots; but he wondered desperately whether the myalls had come and seen his first blundering passage through the water and whether they might not be coming, even now, to gaff him like a fish, a man-fish, helpless under the pink lily blooms.

Mundaru, the buffalo man, was puzzled. He had moved fast and straight through the grasses, and now he was standing on the very spot where his quarry had lain. The marks of him were everywhere: the shape of his body in the mud, the crushed and torn reed-stalks, the place where he had slid into the lagoon. Yet there was no sign of him.

The surface of the pond was clear and unbroken. The green scum in the shallows was neither torn nor disturbed. The blue ducks were swimming placidly, the ripples fanning out in their wake. The egrets stood in elderly contemplation round the verge. A blue king-fisher dipped like a flash of lightning over the pink flowers.

Mundaru squatted on his heels and waited, his eyes darting hither and yon across the shining water and the broad, gleaming stretches of lily leaves. He waited a long time, but no alien sound disturbed the familiar harmony. The swamp-birds fed unruffled and the grasses swayed in unbroken rhythm to the warm wind blowing off the Stone Country. The white man had disappeared completely, as if he were one of those spirit-beings who could hide themselves in the crevice of a rock, or the trunk of a tree, or the hollow of a grass-stalk.

A small chill fear began to creep in on the buffalo man as the leaven of unacknowledged guilt began to work in his subconscious. Perhaps, after all, it was a spirit man. Perhaps the white man was already dead, drowned in the river, and his restless emanation was walking abroad, mocking Mundaru and leading him on to ultimate destruction. Perhaps he was still alive, but using a more potent magic than Mundaru had known or expected. Perhaps this was not white man's magic at all, but the malignant working of Willinja, who had already begun to sing evil against him.

As the fear grew, the guilt thrust itself further and further into his consciousness, until, finally, it was staring him in the face. Like all his people, Mundaru was a believer in the supernatural; and, though he lacked the words to define it, he was facing the dilemma of all believers: the dichotomy between belief and practice, the conflict between tribal discipline and personal desire. By his own act, he had set himself outside the tribe, made himself an outlaw. The channels of strength and sustenance were closed to him for ever. His choice therefore was predetermined. He must go on to complete the killing cycle – be the victim ghost or man. He must survive by his own efforts, live on his own fat, and on the protection of his own totem.

Abruptly, but with a curious, inverted logic, his thoughts turned to Menyan, who was the wife of Willinja. Inside the tribe, she was denied to him, but now, an outlaw, he might take her, if he could, and whether she consented or refused. Afterwards, they could not stay in the tribal lands. But they could flee to the fringe of the white settlement, where other de-tribalised men and women lived a new kind of life, incomplete, but free at least from the threat of ancient sanctions. The thought pleased him. It gave him a new goal, a new, if temporary, courage against the influences working on him from hour to hour.

But first, he must find the white man. . . .

The water was still unbroken. The reed-bed still

whispered in the breeze. Wherever the white man was, he would be heading roughly in the direction of the homestead. His track must lie along the inner bank of the lagoon, nearest to the river and pointing downstream. Mundaru picked up his spears and his killing club and headed off through the reed fringes.

When, a long time later, Dillon broke despairingly out from the lily-beds, the myall had disappeared and there was nothing to show which way he had gone.

Mary Dillon and Sergeant Neil Adams were riding stirrup to stirrup across the red plain, with Billy-Jo a few paces behind them, leading the pack-pony. The heat and the glare and the steady jogging of the horses had reduced them to a drowsy harmony, a laconic familiarity, as if they and their dusky attendant were the only folk left in an empty world. For long stretches, Adams rode in silence, staring straight ahead, absorbed in himself; but, just when it seemed to Mary that he had forgotten or was deliberately ignoring her, he would turn and point out a new thing to interest her – a strange bird, a distorted bottle tree, a pile of fertility stones raised by the aborigines. He had a care for her, an unspoken understanding, and she was grateful to him.

But there was still something that needed to be said, and she put it to him calmly.

'Neil, there's something I want to say to you.'

'Go ahead and say it.'

'You mustn't try to hide anything from me – anything at all.'

He shot her a quick, shrewd glance from under his hat-brim, but his face was in shadow so that she could not see whether he smiled or frowned. Only his voice held a hint of humour.

'I'm not hiding anything, Mary. I don't know anything yet.'

'But you think it's serious, don't you?'

'Any accident is serious in this country, Mary.'

'But you don't believe this is an accident. You think it's blackfellow trouble, don't you?'

'I told you, I'm guessing. I don't know anything.'

'But Lance could be dead . . . killed.'

'He could be. He probably isn't.'

'It might be better if he were.'

The bleakness of the statement staggered him, but he had been long drilled to composure. His eyes never wavered from the vista before him and the ponies continued their steady amble over the plain. After a moment he said quietly:

'Do you want to explain that?'

'There's not much to explain, Neil. We're head over heels in debt to the pastoral company, and they told us last month they wouldn't advance us any more. If the bull is dead, as you think, we're finished – ruined. I don't think Lance could stand that. I'm sure I couldn't.'

'Aren't you under-rating yourself – and him?'

'No. It's the truth.'

They rode on a while in silence, then Adams reined in and said casually:

'Let's rest awhile and cool off.'

He dismounted and came to help her out of the saddle. She was stiff and cramped and she had to hold to him a moment for support. He grinned and said lightly:

'That's nothing to the way you'll feel tomorrow.'

'I'm tougher than you think, Neil.'

'I believe it,' he told her soberly, and moved off to water the horses while she drank greedily from the water-bottle. Later, when they were sitting in the shade and smoking a cigarette before remounting, Adams picked up the thread of their talk. He asked her:

'Do you really think Lance would crack?'

She nodded emphatically.

'Yes. I think it's quite possible. I know him very well, you see. He has great courage, great endurance. But he's too single-minded – too dedicated, if you like. Everything in his life has been subordinated to this ambition of his – even me. He's gambled everything on this breeding project, and he's told me more than once it was his last throw. I believed him. I still do. There are people like that, you know, Neil. So long as the goal is clear and possible, they can take anything. But when the goal is unclear or beyond them – they snap. Lance is a man like that.'

'And you?'

His eyes were hooded, but she caught the undertone of irony in the question. Her answer was blunt.

'I'm one of those who survive by walking away and cutting their losses.'

'You'd walk away from Lance?'

'From the country first. But from Lance, too, if he insisted on staying. I'd already made up my mind to do it before this happened.'

If the answer shocked him, he gave no sign, but looked at her with level eyes and said:

'Don't you love him, Mary?'

'Enough to be honest with him – yes. But not enough to stay and let this blasted country wear out everything that was good between us. Does that shock you, Neil?'

He shrugged and gave her a sardonic sidelong grin.

'Nothing ever shocks a policeman. Besides, it's a pleasure to meet an honest witness. If you've finished your cigarette, we'd better move. I want to get to the ridges before sunset.'

He turned, and began walking away towards the horses, but her voice stayed him.

'Neil?'

'Yes?'

She moved to face him, her eyes cool and challenging.

'One question, Neil. What odds will you give me on Lance being alive?'

He chewed on the question a moment, then answered it flatly:

'At this moment, even money. But the odds might be better on the course. . . . Come on, let's ride.'

But the longer they rode, the more the question

nagged at him: which way did she want the odds – longer or shorter? And which way did he want them himself?

Willinja, the scorcerer, was waiting for the buffalo men to complete their ritual preparations and present themselves to him, ready for the kill. He, too, had his own dilemmas of time, circumstance and responsibility.

Like all the initiates of the animistic cults, he was a man of singular intelligence and imagination. In any society he would have risen to eminence and the exercise of power. The whole history and tradition of his tribe was stored and tabulated in his memory. He knew all its chants and all its rituals, many of them hours long and all of them intricate.

The complex relationships of tribe and totem, of marriage and generation – the whole codex of human and animal relationships was as clear to him as the legal canons to a twentieth-century jurist. He was pharmacist, physician, psychologist – and within the limits of his knowledge and experience, good in each capacity. He was priest and augur, diplomat and judge in equity. Behind his broad receding forehead he carried relatively more knowledge than any four men in a twentieth-century society. More than most men, he understood social responsibility. He, and others like him, held the tribal life together and maintained it in a workable pattern against the constant tendency to disintegration.

This, in effect, was his problem now. He had ordered a killing: in the tribal code, a legal killing. But the legal process would fail of its effect if Mundaru killed the white man first. Adamidji, the white policeman, would see two crimes instead of one, and the punishment would be all the greater. Even tribal killings were forbidden by the white man's law, and so, he could not explain, in any intelligible fashion, his effort at prevention and punishment. There were things the white man would never understand: like the exchange of wives to satisfy a quarrel, or to show hospitality; like the payment of blood for blood, and the need to keep certain things secret under penalty of death.

When a man stole another's wife, or took to himself a woman of the wrong totem, the white man gave him sanctuary and protected him against the spears of the avengers. He impeded the course of age-old justice. When, in the old days, he drove a tribe out of its own preserves into a new territory – even a better one – he did not understand that he was signing the death-warrant of the social unit. There was no bridge between these two worlds – no concordance between their ethics and philosophies.

So, in this moment of crisis, Willinja must work alone, according to his own knowledge and tradition, a Stone Age Atlas, carrying the weight of his world on his own ageing shoulders.

From the shadowy recesses of a cave in the kangaroo rock the buffalo men came out, limping from the recent ordeal. Their feet were shod with the kadaitja boots – made of emu feathers and the fur of kangaroos and daubed with blood drawn from their own arms. When they walked they would not leave footprints like ordinary men – because until the act was done, they were not ordinary men any more. Even the spears they carried were special to the occasion.

When they came to Willinja they stood before him, heads bowed, eyes downcast, waiting his commands. They were crisp and clear, but ritually careful. Time was important. If possible Mundaru must be killed before he killed the white man.

The manner of the killing was equally important. He must be speared from behind – in the middle of the back. The spear must be withdrawn and a flake of sharp quartz, representing the spirit snake, must be inserted to eat the liver fat. The wound must be sealed and cauterised with a hot stone, and Mundaru, bleeding internally, with the spirit snake eating his entrails, must be driven forward until he died in his tracks. No woman or child must see the act or the death. The man who threw the spear must never be named, because this was a communal act, absolved from all revenge or the penalty of blood.

Did they understand it all? Yes. Did they understand that if they failed they too lay under threat of death? Yes.

He dismissed them curtly and stood a long time, watching their swift, limping run towards the river. Then he picked up his instruments of magic, wrapped them carefully in a bundle of paper-bark and strode back to the encampment.

The women were beginning to straggle back, loaded with yams and lily-bulbs and wooden dishes full of wild honey, but Menyan was not among them, and Willinja waited, puzzled at first and then uneasy, for the arrival of his youngest wife.

CHAPTER FIVE

IT WAS LATE afternoon when they reached the sandstone escarpment and pushed their tired horses through
the gorge into the valley. The kites were still wheeling
round the carcase of the bull and they rose in screaming, flapping clouds as the riders approached. The air
was heavy with carrion smell, and Mary Dillon gagged
desperately and reined in while Adams and Billy-Jo
rode forward to examine the kill.

She saw them dismount, examine the kill and then
begin casting the ground for tracks. They were like
figures in a lunar landscape of raw colours, harsh contours and long, distorted shadows; but they moved her
to sudden and vivid resentment. The males were in
council. The woman must wait their pleasure, no
matter how deeply she might be involved in the outcome.

Then she noticed a curious thing: the whole emphasis
and balance of the tableau seemed to have changed.
Although Billy-Jo was kneeling in the dust and Adams
standing above him, it was the black man who was
suddenly in command.

All the way from the homestead, she had hardly
noticed him. He had that attitude of effacement, which
the aborigine effects in the presence of the white man –
a kind of grey, faintly-smiling acquiescence in whatever the white boss chose to do. He was no longer

young. His hair was grey and his face deeply lined. He wore riding-boots, denims and patched shirt of check cotton. His shoulders stooped as if he were ashamed of being seen in the white man's cast-offs. But here, in this wild landscape, he seemed to take on new stature and authority. His gestures were ample and expressive. When he spoke, Adams listened attentively; and when he stood up, his shadow fell giant-like along the dust.

In spite of her fatigue and ill-humour, she edged her horse closer to follow their talk. Before she had gone a dozen paces, Adams looked up and yelled at her:

'Stay where you are! We're having enough trouble. The stockboys have walked all over the ground.'

She was parched, dusty and aching in every muscle. This male brusqueness was the last straw. She propped the pony hard on his hindquarters and yelled back:

'It's my husband you're looking for! Just remember I'm interested!'

He did not answer, but threw her an ironic salute and bent again to talk to Billy-Jo, who, crouched like a scenting dog, was moving away towards the far end of the valley.

As quickly as it had risen, her irritation subsided and she felt small, foolish and regretful. Loneliness invaded her – a sense of failure and inadequacy, as though she were built to breathe a grosser air, to demand a sicklier nurture than these sturdy, inland people. She felt like an exotic fish in a glass bowl, envious of the free life of the river reaches. It was the old problem in a new shape; but this time there was no Lance to blame for it. There was only Mary Dillon, cross-grained and saddle-sore, a nuisance to others and a singular disappointment to herself.

Twenty minutes later Adams and Billy-Jo finished their circuit of the valley, remounted and rode back to join her. Adams's face was clouded with concern and his voice was oddly gentle.

'Sorry to keep you standing about, Mary. We had some trouble picking up the tracks.'

Billy-Jo grinned at her in deprecation.

'Stockmen stupid, Missus. Walkabout all over. Kick up ground alla same cattle muster.'

'But you did find what you wanted, Neil?'

He nodded gravely.

'It's clear enough, Mary. The myalls were in the valley. Five, six, maybe more. They speared the bull, then broke his hind legs with clubs. They made a fire over there and cooked some of the meat.'

'And Lance?'

'Lance was here too. His pony has a worn hind shoe. He came in at a gallop, and there are two spots where the pony reared. He must have caught the myalls in the act.'

'And they wounded him – is that it?'

'It looks like it. The tracks show that he galloped through the valley, then out again. It looks as though he was wounded by a spear, because he wasn't thrown or pulled out of the saddle.'

Shame and a sharp cold fear took hold of her. Her voice trembled as she asked:

'What happened then?'

'We don't know. We'll pick up his tracks at the

mouth of the gorge and just follow from there. The stockboys may have found something, but from the way they've been blundering round in here, I doubt it.'

They rode on in silence for a few moments while she digested this proposition, then she said in a small voice:

'Neil, I'm sorry I was a nuisance. I'm scared and edgy.'

He turned and grinned at her in his quirky, sardonic fashion.

'It's a woman's privilege, Mary. You're doing fine. Just try to relax a little. Billy-Jo's the best tracker from Broome to Normanton. We'll know something soon. There's still an hour and a half of daylight.'

'Neil?'

'Yes, Mary?'

'What are the odds now?'

He frowned, considering the question, then he answered frankly:

'They've shortened a bit, Mary. All this happened twenty-four hours ago. We don't know how badly Lance was wounded, or how much he was hurt by the fall. There's only one thing that tips the odds in our favour. He can't be very far away.'

The answer seemed to satisfy her, and he was content to leave it incomplete. There was no point in telling her the other things that he and Billy-Jo had found: the ochre dust and the charcoal sticks and the animal fur, with which one of the myalls had been daubed, in preparation for a new killing.

. . . . . .

When Lance Dillon crawled out of the water and back into the reeds, he was in an extremity of weakness. He was chattering with cold; his skin was crinkled and pulpy; one shoulder and breast was throbbing with pain, and his limbs were shaken with uncontrollable, spastic tremors. He lay face downward on the ground, gasping for breath and fighting desperately to clear his mind of the fever mists which were the prelude to helpless delirium.

He knew now, with absolute conviction, that unaided he could never reach the homestead alive. The infection in his shoulder was spreading and his strength was running out much faster than he could maintain it with the meagre, vegetable diet available to him. The least effort was a dangerous expense, which soon would become fatal.

He closed his eyes and tried to direct his vagrant mind to an assessment of his situation. The appearance of the aircraft meant only one thing: Mary had understood that he was in trouble and had summoned help. Even now they would be out looking for him. He tried to add the hours he had been wandering, the hours it would take mounted men to reach the area. But even this simple calculation was beyond him, and he slipped off in a dozing day-dream of Mary, of faceless horsemen, of aircraft turning into birds and circling above his own dead body.

The dream faded back to reality, and brief reason told him that he must get out of the high grasses and head back to the river, where at least he might have a chance of meeting the searchers. Here in the swamp-reaches he was buried, as if in a green tomb, and if the myalls had missed him the chances of being found by his friends were reduced to nothing. The waving stalks would cover him until he rotted into their roots.

The thought gave him a deceptive consolation. He need not run any more, need not fear any more. He had simply to sink down and let the grass swallow him like the sea. As if in confirmation of the thought, a schoolboy tag floated up into memory. . . .

'Where the green swell is in the havens dumb,
    And out of the swing of the sea.'

The rhythm of it rocked him soothingly. The voices of the cicadas sank to an undulating drone. He felt himself slipping into a warm deep, like a waterlogged leaf, until a sharp spasm of pain jerked him back to consciousness.

This was the way death would come – an insidious luxury, robbing him of will. This was more dangerous than the myall spears. He must summon his strength and fight it. He looked up, trying to gauge the direction of the sun from the tangled shadows of the grass. It was afternoon. The sun was on his right, so the river must lie straight ahead of him. Now or never, he must begin to move.

Slowly, foot by painful foot, he began to drag himself slug-like along the ground, among the green-white stalks, whose crowns waved infinitely high above his head.

· · · · · · ·

Menyan, who was named for the moon, and who was the youngest wife of Willinja the sorcerer, was digging yams on the river-flat. She was alone, which was unusual, because usually the women worked in groups or under the care of an old man, to keep them safe from the wandering bucks who sometimes tried to seduce them from their husbands. Except for a small pubic tassel of kangaroo fur, she was completely naked, and she squatted on her haunches prising up the long brown tubers with a pointed stick. It was an easy labour. The ground was soft and the ripe yams grew close to the surface; so that her thoughts wandered and she was able to enjoy the rare privacy and the warmth of the westering sun on her skin.

By the white man's measure, she was fifteen years of age, and she had been married to Willinja from the time of her first period, but so far she was childless. Her breasts were still small, her belly flat, and there was no sign of the pain or the swelling, which the older women told her were the signs that a child had been dreamed into her.

This was the reason for her working alone. The older women had made fun of her. Willinja's other wives had mocked her as barren and useless, until she had quarrelled with them and wandered off to escape their taunts. She knew as well as they did that it was not her fault, that old men did not make so many children as young ones; but the stigma was still there and she resented it deeply.

Tribally and personally, she was incomplete. Just as a man was not fully initiated until he had been

86

circumcised and passed through fire and taken a woman to wife, so the woman was not fully admitted to the secret life until she had given birth to a child.

Some women, she knew, had made a quick progress to this last initiation. They had lovers who dreamed children into them in secret, or after the last dances of a big corrobboree. Some were lent as wives to a relative or in payment of a debt, and from these unions a child came sometimes more quickly than from an old husband. But so far, Willinja had kept her exclusively to himself, and she was afraid of the far sight with which the spirit men had endowed him.

Yet, all in all, she was not too unhappy. She was still child enough to throw off cares quickly, and still woman enough to hope that one day a young man might come to buy her from Willinja, or 'pull' her from him in the conventional elopement which might be absolved later by the payment of a suitable price. If she could choose – and choice was limited for a tribal woman – she would prefer Mundaru, the buffalo man.

There was a vitality about him, an urgent strength, that set him apart from the other bucks. He wanted her badly. Given the opportunity, he would try to take her. But now she knew she could not surrender to him. What the men did or said in their secret places was a forbidden mystery; but the women understood well enough that Mundaru had been named an outcast to be cut off for ever from the tribal communion. A woman might dare her husband's anger to join herself with a younger man; but few would dare the interdict of the tribe. To mate with Mundaru now would be like mating with a dead man.

The thought chilled her and she turned away from it. There were other man who desired her and who might yet be bold enough to take her. She began to sing softly the song which the women used to call their lovers to them. Suddenly, there was a rustle in the grasses behind her. A shadow fell across her naked back, and on the warm soil under her hands. She looked up. Her eyes dilated, her mouth opened in a soundless scream as Mundaru, painted and armed for the kill, advanced towards her.

When they reached the mouth of the gorge, Billy-Jo dismounted and walked ahead, casting about for the tracks of Dillon's pony among the newer prints made by the stockboys. Adams and Mary Dillon sat watching him while the ponies dropped their heads and began cropping the sparse tussocks at their feet. Adams mopped his face, took a couple of sips from the water-bottle and handed it across to Mary.

'A thing to notice, Mary . . .' He pointed across to Billy-Jo. 'Billy-Jo has kept his primitive skills. The stockboys have lost theirs. They don't have to depend on them any more to stay alive. They're half-way into our world, but they've lost foothold in their own.'

She looked at him sharply.

'Are you stating a fact, Neil, or pointing a moral?'

'Read it any way you like,' he shrugged off the challenge.

'It's still true. It's the secret of living in a country like this. Make the earth your ally and you can survive. Make it an enemy and you're fighting a running battle that you must lose in the end.'

'I've lost mine, if that's what you mean.'

'I wasn't thinking of you, Mary.' His voice grew grave. 'I was thinking of Lance. Back in the valley he was wounded – how badly we don't know. Somewhere out there between the river and the trees, he dismounted or was thrown. . . .'

'Or finished off by the myalls.'

'That too.' He nodded a sober agreement. 'But if he escaped, then his survival depends in part on his own physical condition and in part on knowledge and his sympathy with the country. It's a good area hereabout. There's the river and the grassland and the timber. Lots of game, lots of food, if you know where to find it.'

'Lance used to say the same thing. I – I think he knows.'

A hundred yards away, Billy-Jo raised his hand in signal then pointed away towards the paper-barks. Adams waved an acknowledgment and they trotted over towards the black-tracker. Adams frowned in puzzlement and asked more of himself than of Mary:

'I wonder why he headed that way, away from the homestead?'

It was Billy-Jo who supplied the first, tentative answer.

'Wounded man, tired horse, both need water. Maybe make for river, maybe for shade under trees.'

Still walking, he led them step by step towards the paper-bark fringe, but before they reached it they saw the stockboys ride out, churning up the dust in a hand-gallop. Adams swore softly when he saw that they had not yet found Dillon, then he reined in and waited for them.

Mary gave a small gasp of fear when she saw that Jimmy, the head-boy, had Dillon's hat hung on his pommel. He handed it to Adams and then made his report in tumbling, liquid pidgin.

'Catchim tracks in timber. Horse belong boss Dillon, tired, walkim slow. Hat he come off, boss-Dillon maybe sick. Catchim more tracks by river grass. Man lie there long time, bleed much. More tracks go down to river. We leave. Come back longa Adamidji.'

Adams listened until he had finished, then explained it quickly to Mary.

'They picked up your husband's hat in the timber, where they found his tracks. They followed them into the grasses and came to the spot where he must have been thrown, then they came back to meet us.'

'Didn't he say something about blood?'

Adams dismissed it curtly

'He must have lain there some time. We know he was wounded. That would explain the blood.'

'What are you going to do now?'

'Get Jimmy to take us there. We'll set the other boys working to clear a landing-strip on the open ground.

90

Gilligan's flying back this way tomorrow morning. Wait here a while.'

He began a swift explanation to the stockboys, and after a few moments he rode off with them towards the open plain at the foot of the ridges, leaving her alone with Billy-Jo. The old man watched her a moment with shrewd, sidelong eyes, then said tentatively:

'Sergeant good man, missus. See much, say little, trustim sure.'

'I know, Billy-Jo. But I'm worried about my husband.'

The old man shrugged and scuffed his feet in the dust.

'Missus young. Catchim new husband, makim piccaninny longtime yet.'

She flushed and threw him a quick look, but his head was bowed and his dusky face hidden under his hat-brim. It was no new thought to her, but uttered by a stranger in bastard tongue, it had a new and shocking impact. She turned and stared away across the red plain where Adams was pacing off the rough strip and showing the stockboys how to clear it with their bare hands and with branches broken from the scrub timber.

She was drawn to him. So much was easy to admit; but what drew her harder to name. An ease, perhaps? A confidence in the way he wore the world – as if it were a sprigged waistcoat instead of a hair shirt. He was a man in equilibrium, stable and content; whereas Lance, for all his strength and driving power, seemed always in conflict. Neil Adams made no demands on life, and yet life seemed to pattern itself in order about him. Lance was always restless, prescient, as if building, all too slowly, a rampart against chaos.

Was this, perhaps, the nub of the matter? That she was dissatisfied with the man she had, and wanted another; that the land had taken on the colour of her own wintry discontent? Would it look more like Eden, if she were travelling it with Neil Adams?

When she saw him galloping back with Jimmy, the stockman, she dismissed the thought abruptly, lest he read it in her eyes. If Lance were dead, she would have the right to nourish it, but if not . . . She had a vision of him, spread-eagled in the sun, the life bleeding out of him; and once again she was bitterly ashamed of herself.

The shadows were lengthening as they rode into the timber, with the stockman leading, and Billy-Jo following, intent on the signs. When they broke out on the paper-barks and came to the grass patch where Dillon had been thrown, they dismounted. The stockman held the horses, while Billy-Jo and Adams made their examination, with Mary a pace behind them, watching intently.

This time, Adams was more careful of her. As the tracker read the signs, he translated them crisply.

'This is where he was thrown. You see how the grass was broken and the ground hollowed a little by the impact. He lay some time, bleeding . . . then apparently got up and walked away, using a stick. . . . There are no trees hereabouts, so it looks as though it might be a spear he's using. From here he headed down to the river. . . . That's natural, because he'd be thirsty from loss of blood and body fluids. It's a good sign because it shows he's thinking straight and seeing straight. . . .'

He broke off as Billy-Jo called his attention to new signs; a wisp of fur, a faint smear on a grass-stalk, a depression in the swampy earth. She saw him frown and then mutter something to the tracker. Then she questioned him sharply:

'Something new, Neil? What is it?'

He straightened and faced her. His eyes were hard, but his voice was carefully controlled.

'The myalls came this way too, Mary. It must have been afterwards, because there's no sign of a struggle. But they were very close on his tracks.'

'How long ago?'

'At a guess, this time yesterday.'

'That makes it twenty-four hours.'

'Near enough.'

'You can say all that, just from looking at the ground?'

'I can't. But Billy-Jo can. The little I know confirms it.'

'That means Lance is dead, doesn't it?'

For the life of him, he could not tell whether a wish or a fear prompted the question. He shook his head.

'Not yet. It just means that the odds on his survival have shortened again.'

He turned to the stockman. 'Jimmy, you head back and join the others. Keep 'em working until dark;

93

then make camp and start on the strip again at sunrise. We'll push on and I'll get word to you before Gilligan arrives. Is that clear?'

'All clear, boss.' He touched his hat to Mary and rode off, as casually as if he were going to a muster. Adams watched him go, then handed Mary the bridles of the ponies.

'You lead 'em, Mary. I want to stay close to Billy-Jo. We'll go on tracking as long as the light lasts.'

'And after that?'

But Adams was already three paces ahead, following Billy-Jo through the long grasses towards the river.

Five miles away, the kadaitja men, limping in their feather boots, had reached the river, and were fanning out over the flats to begin the hunt for Mundaru. They were in pain, but the pain was an ever-present reminder of the sacred character of their mission. It was more than this, for the burnt and dislocated toes had now become magical eyes to guide their steps towards their quarry. They walked in two worlds, infused with supernatural power, but still applying the simple pragmatic rules of the hunter: stealth, concealment, calculation.

Their calculation was simple but sound. If the white man were still alive it was because he was using the abundant cover of the swamp-land. If he were dead, Mundaru would first hide the body and then use the same swamp-lands to provide himself with food. He would not risk a break into open country during the daylight hours.

There was no doubt in their minds that Mundaru knew of the sentence promulgated against him. This was the whole virtue of projective magic, that the victim sensed it, felt it in his body long before the moment of execution. The knowledge would weaken and confuse him, so that he would become an easier prey. More than this, they knew that the white men were out. They had seen the plane and the dust-clouds kicked up by the horses. They gauged, accurately, that the white men would follow the tracks from the valley to the river, so that they would end by driving Mundaru down-stream towards the sacred spears.

The spearmen were hidden from each other and spread over a mile of country, but they moved in perfect co-ordination. Their communication was a cryptic mimicry of animal noises: the raucous cry of a cockatoo, the honk of a swamp-goose, the thudding resonant beat which a kangaroo makes with his tail on the ground, the high-rising whistle of a whip-bird. The sounds were never repeated in the same sequence nor from the same location, so that even the wariest listener would hardly suspect their origin.

Towards the end, Mundaru would hear and understand, but then it would be too late. The kadaitja men would be circling and closing in on him. There would be a silence, long and terrible; and out of the silence would come the throbbing note of the bull-roarer – the tjuringa, the sacred wood or stone, which is pierced with holes so that when it is twirled in the air, it roars deeply in the voice of the dream-time people. To Mundaru it would be a death chant, and before its last echoes died he would fall to the sacred spear-thrust.

But all this was still far ahead of them. It was ordained, but it was not inevitable. It still depended on their own skill, and on the use each man made of the magic with which he had been endowed. So they moved silently, every sense prickling, up-stream towards their victim.

CHAPTER SIX

THE RIVER slept shade-dappled under the late sun.
The sound of it was a whispered counterpoint to the
creek of palm leaves and the crepitant buzz of insects.

They came to it on foot, leaving the horses tethered
on the high bank, and while Billy-Jo began scouting
the sandy verge, Neil Adams and Mary Dillon waited
together, watching the play of shadows and the
jewelled flight of a kingfisher across the water.

The weariness of the long ride was in their bones,
and Mary felt her courage thinning out with the
decline of the day. Her face was drawn and dust-
marked. Her eyes burned with the glare. Every muscle
was aching from unaccustomed hours in the saddle.
Adams, too, was tired; she saw it in the deep lines
about his mouth, the droop of his shoulders and the
slackness of his strong, hard hands. Yet his attitude
was one of relaxation and not of tension. He was alert
and watchful as ever, and she envied him his leathery
strength while she resented his seeming indifference
to her own condition. The resentment put an edge on
her voice as she questioned him:

'What have you found, Neil? What are you thinking? You've hardly spoken a word for the last half-
hour.'

To her surprise, he was instantly apologetic.

'I'm sorry, Mary. I'm not used to company on the job – certainly not women's company. Billy-Jo and I don't need many words, we think in harmony.'

'And I'm an intruder, is that it?'

He grinned at her, disarmingly.

'No. Just a figure in the landscape that I haven't had time to notice. Besides, there's not much to tell that you don't know already. Your husband reached the river at this point. The myalls were on his tracks. We still don't know how far they were behind him. All this happened twenty-four hours ago, you see, and the ground dries quickly in the sunlight. The two sets of tracks look as though they were made at the same time – although we know they weren't.'

'You're trying to tell me they caught Lance?'

'It's possible – yes.'

A cold finger of fear probed at her heart-strings, but her voice was steady as she questioned him again.

'He could be dead by now – is that it?'

'He could . . . but he may not be. If I were you I'd prepare myself for the worst – and still hope for the best.'

Once again the calm containment of her shocked him. She said simply:

'I'm prepared. You needn't be afraid of me.'

He gave her a shrewd, sidelong look and said dryly:

'You have a lot of courage, Mary.'

'More than you expected?'

The question was barbed, but he shrugged it off.

'Maybe. But I'm glad, anyway. Whatever happens, you're going to need it.'

Swift anger took hold of her and she blazed at him:

'You're very practised in brutality, aren't you? I suppose that's what makes you a good policeman.'

Before he had time to frame a reply, Billy-Jo came hurrying towards them along the sandy bank, his dark weathered face set in a frown of puzzlement. Adams questioned him sharply:

'Find anything?'

The tracker pointed along the bank, up-stream and down from the point where they stood:

'Blackfellow tracks all about. Walkim up and down. Makeim fire, eat and sleep. No tracks for white boss. No clothes, no blood, nothing.'

A gleam of admiration brightened in Adams's eyes. More to himself than to Mary, he muttered:

'Clever boy. He used the river to break his tracks. Must have been far enough ahead to throw them completely off the scent. I wonder which way he was heading?'

His eyes searched the farther bank, where the steep, muddy incline was tufted with thorn-bush and creeper and the tangled, water-hungry roots of the pandanus palms. Mary Dillon watched him intently, not daring to intrude again on the patient privacy of his thoughts. It was Billy-Jo who spoke the first word; quietly but with the authority of complete understanding.

'Loseim light fast, boss. Maybe we cross river and look around, eh?'

Adams pondered a moment, then nodded gravely and turned to Mary.

'We'll have to leave you for a while, Mary. There's

99

swamp-land on the other side and we'd like to make a quick survey before dark. Bring the horses down here, water them and then tether them. Then you could start collecting wood for a fire. There's a rifle in my saddle-bucket. There's no danger, but if you want us in a hurry fire two shots. We'll be back by dark.'

The words were already on her tongue to tell him that she knew nothing about handling horses, that she had never fired a rifle in her life, that whenever they had camped, it was Lance or the stockboys who had gathered the firewood, that her flesh crept at the sight of an insect and that the terror of emptiness haunted her like the beginning of madness. The words were there, but she choked them back and said only:

'You go ahead. Don't worry about me. I'll have a meal ready when you come back.'

For the first time in their day-long company, Adams's lean face relaxed into a smile of genuine approval. He patted her shoulder and said gently:

'Good girl! We won't be gone long. We may have better news for you when we come back.'

He turned away, and with Billy-Jo at his heels walked down-stream to where the river narrowed and the water ran swiftly over a stony outcrop where they could cross without fear of crocodiles. Mary Dillon watched them until they scrambled into the bushes of the farther bank; then, alone, scared yet oddly elated, she walked back to untether the horses and bring them down to drink at the river.

As the tired animals drooped their muzzles into the

water, she unsaddled them, awkwardly, yet with a curious satisfaction in the simple labour. Always before she had avoided it, as if it were some kind of concession to the hated country. Now she was happy to do it, at the casual behest of a man who challenged her with mockery instead of love. It was a bleak commentary on her relation with Lance, a terse query on her attitude to Neil Adams. She resented him, but she was eager to please him. She wanted to hurt him, but when she found him beyond the reach of her ill-temper she did violence to herself to earn his off-hand praise.

Not once in three years of marriage had she conceded half so much to her husband, who might even now be lying dead and staring with blind eyes at the peach-bloom sky. In this last hour of the day, with perception heightened to feverish clarity by fatigue and resentment, she understood how far she had failed him and how much he, in his own fashion, had failed her. He had loved her, but love was not enough. He had set her too high, conceded her too much, handled her too gently. He lacked the perceptive brutality of Neil Adams; the egotism, the cool certainty of ultimate conquest. Even now, fear for him as she might, she could weigh his death for profit and loss as if he were alien from her life.

Strange that here in the narrow solitude of the river valley, she could face the thought without shame – if not without regret.

When the horses had drunk their fill, she hitched them to a palm-bole near the embankment and began to walk slowly along the bank, gathering driftwood and branches for the fire. Each armful she gathered took her a little farther from the horses and the rifle. Each return took a little longer in the paling light. At first she was nervous; her eyes searched this way and that among the shadows of the undergrowth, her head full of nameless terrors. Then the tension in her relaxed slowly, so that a moment came when she thought suddenly: I am not afraid; I am alone, but not afraid. There is water and sand and rock and trees ruffling in the wind, but I walk as if in a familiar place. The terrors are elsewhere – with Lance, with Billy-Jo, with Adams; but not with me.

By the time she had finished, the driftwood was piled high on the sand, and she was hot, filthy and uncomfortable. She looked about for a spot to wash herself and found, twenty yards up-stream, a small rock-pool. It was deep, ringed by scored sandstone, clear as crystal over a sandy bottom where small speckled fish swam in a low slant of sunlight. She felt it with her hand. It still held the warmth of the day. Without a second thought, she stripped off her clothes, spread them carefully on the rock shelf and stepped into the water, sliding down into it until it covered her breasts and lapped the hollow of her throat.

The touch of it was like silk on her parched skin. The weariness and the saddle-ache drifted off her like the dust of the red plains so that she seemed to float, a new creature, slack, content, invulnerable, in a strange new element. The tree-shadows lengthened and lay weightless across her body, the peach-bloom sky darkened slowly to crimson, the chorus of cicadas ragged and scattered, the first spasmodic cool of the evening came ruffling along the river-reaches, but she still lay there, lapped in the waters of this illusory baptism, until from far across the river she heard Billy-Jo hailing:

'. . . Dillon. . . . Boss Dillon. . . !'

And then, more distant, the long despairing ululation of Adams's voice:

'Dillon! . . . Answer me! Where are you? Dillon!'

Mundaru, the buffalo man, heard it too – so close that he could see through the stalks of the grass, the trunk of the shouting man. A single leap and a single spear thrust would silence the shout for ever: but Mandaru squatted, motionless as a rabbit in the depths of the grass until the man and the voice had passed far beyond him. This was not his victim. To kill him would profit nothing. Besides, he was tired now from the day's stalking, from hunger, and from the long, violent ravishing of Menyan.

It was a thing he had not counted on: her terror, her cowering rejection of him, as if he were unclean or a threatening spirit man. Withdrawal, yes – a token flight, an ultimate surrender – this was the ritual of a tribal abduction when a young wife was 'pulled' from an ageing husband. The woman must prove fidelity before she could be unfaithful. The man must prove strength before he could possess another man's woman.

But Menyan's reaction had been quite different: a panic horror, the desperate bone-breaking struggles of a trapped bird; so that in the end he had to stifle her and beat her savagely before he took her. Only afterward, in the hour of staleness and disgust, did he understand the reason: Menyan knew what he himself had only suspected. The tribe had ranged itself against him. They had pointed the bone at him and sung him to death. Already the executioners were on his traces.

So now he sat crouched in the six-foot grasses, listening to the retreating voices of the white man, listening for the sounds that would herald the coming of the kadaitja men and clinging to his last tenuous hope: that he might find his own victim, eat his liver fat and arm himself against the magic of the tribal avengers. If he failed in this, he was lost and he might as well lie down and die in his tracks.

He had not much time. Night was coming down on the land. He must spend it alone, without fire or company, in a last desperate search for his victim. He clasped his hands round his knees and let his head drop forward, lapsing like an animal into fitful sleep while far voices rang above the clatter of the evening insects.

'Dillon! . . . Where are you? Dillon. . . !'

The kadaitja men heard it too and they froze, their painted faces pointing like the muzzles of hounds towards the sound. They did not understand the words, but their import was clear: the white men were out looking for their lost brother. The white man might be dead or alive – it made small matter. But those who were seeking him were a danger, a possible impediment to a ritual act necessary for the safety of the tribe. If they came upon Mundaru first, they would take him away, beyond the reach of the sacred spears. But since they were still shouting, they had not found him yet. Somewhere in the long, undulant stretches of grass, higher than the head of the tallest man, he was hiding. He could not break out now. He must spend the night in the swamp. In the darkness he would be blind and beset by spirits. They themselves had no fear of the dark because of the potent magic with which they were armed and because of the all-seeing eye planted in their small toes under the feathered boots.

So they waited, rigid and alert for the signal from their leader which would tell them what to do. Ahead of them the cries continued awhile then stopped. Out of the silence they heard the signal – the cry of a whip-bird, once, twice and again. They moved forward slowly, parting the grasses as the wind might part them, rhythmically, without damage to leaf or stalk-fibre.

Distant but clear, the shouting began again, but this time on a new note, sharp and urgent:

'Billy-Jo! Over here! Hurry, man, hurry!'

Lance Dillon heard it, as he had heard all the others, through the whirling confusion of fever. Like the rest, it meant nothing to him but a new, shapeless nightmare against which the tired mechanism of his brain struggled continuously as he made his sluggish, reptilian progress through the grass-roots.

In these last dragging hours he had learned many lessons: that time is relative, that there is a climax to pain, and after that, a numbness; that sick men see visions, that reason is a razor-path, with darkness on one side and a howling madness on the other, that once a man topples off into darkness there is only the blind compulsion of the will urging him forward to a goal once clearly seen but now lost, like a beacon quenched in the storm-wind.

It was the will that drove the tired heart and kept the sick blood pumping round the circuit of arteries and veins and capillaries. It was the will that kept the hands clawing, one after the other, trailing the body after them like a bloated bladder. The will gave sight to eyes puffed and glued with suppuration; it stifled the screaming agony of sunburn and insect poison; it fought off nightmares and shouted down the siren voices that urged him to lie down and sleep, to stand up and dare the spears, to weep for pity in this pitiless land.

Yet there was a limit to what the will could do. One by one, the instruments at its command were wearing out . . . flesh and muscle and blood and the marrow that kept the bones alive. One by one they would refuse their functions until the driving dynamo which is the core of a man seized up and shuddered to a standstill.

Lance Dillon was beyond reason, but the final syllogism of his last logical thinking was etched deep in the cortex of his brain. He must keep moving. All else was illusion – a swamp-fire luring him to destruction. So he paid no heed to the voices calling his name and kept dragging himself forward. But being part-blind, he did not see that the sun was standing in the wrong position and that every movement was taking him farther from the river and his rescuers.

Darkness came down at a single stride, and Mary Dillon piled more wood on the fire, so that the flames leaped up to make a small island of light on the sand. She could not begin to cook until the blaze had died into coals, but she needed the warmth and the radiance to hold at bay the new terrors of the night. For a long time now, there had been no shouting, no human sound at all – only the whisper of the water, the spasmodic clamour of birds settling themselves to roost, the clump of a leaping wallaby, the squeak and chitter of bats dipping out of the shadows across the star-spotted water.

Never in her life had she felt so lonely. She wanted to scream at the top of her voice for Adams and Billy-Jo, but she feared the echo that might come mocking out of the wilderness. Tags from old bushmen's tales distorted themselves into nightmares that lurked just outside the ring of firelight: the bunyip monster who lived in dark pools, the headless stockman of the Stone Country, the totem crocodile who picked his teeth with a hairpin and ate a white woman every birthday, the mad Duke of Kilparinga, heir to an English title, who ran crazy with an axe because he caught leprosy from a native girl. In another time, she had laughed them off as follies told by simple men in outback bars, but here on the river verge, they were suddenly monstrous and real.

To divert herself she began unstrapping the packs and laying out the food and the utensils. The tin plates fell from her hands with a clatter. The startled horses whinnied and from the leaves over her head a bird squawked and flapped away into the night. She threw herself on the sand and covered her face with her hands.

Then away down-stream she heard the sound of men splashing through the water and the merciful echo of Adams's voice. Sick with relief and shame, she gathered up the fallen plates and began to make a brave show of preparing the meal. But when Adams and Billy-Jo stepped into the light, she had a new shock. Billy-Jo was carrying, slung over his shoulders, the limp body of a native girl. Adams's face was drawn, his mouth tight as a trap, he said curtly:

'We found her over by the swamp, she's in a bad way. Put her down, Billy-Jo.'

The tracker laid the dark, childish body down on the sand and Mary gasped when she saw the extent of the injuries. The face had been battered to a bloody pulp. The breasts were torn, as if by animal claws and the narrow flanks were covered with blood. She was alive but her breathing was shallow and irregular. Mary looked at Adams with startled eyes.

'Who is she? What happened to her?'

'Beaten and raped. She's married, the pubic covering shows that. She was gathering food away from the other women. Whoever did it must have surprised her. She fought and this happened. That's all we know.'

'She's only a child.'

'They marry young in these parts.'

'It's horrible . . . horrible.' Mary turned away as the nausea gripped her. Adams bent over the small broken body, examining it with clinical care. Without turning, he called sharply:

'Mary! Bring me a water-bottle and the whisky.'

When they were brought, he raised the girl's head and forced a few drops of raw spirit into her broken mouth, then he laid her back on the sand and stood up, shaking his head.

'She'll die tonight. I'd like to get a word or two out of her before she goes. See if you can clean her up a little, then cover her with blankets and start bathing her face.'

Mary hesitated a moment, then without a word turned away to get blankets and a towel from the saddle-packs. Adams followed her and laid a tentative hand on her shoulder. He said wearily:

'I'm sorry, Mary, I haven't anything to tell you about your husband. It might take us half a day to pick up his tracks in the grass over there.'

He ran his hand through his thick hair in a gesture of puzzlement.

'The girl's tied in with this somewhere but I can't see how just yet. It's possible that the man who raped her is the man who is hunting your husband.'

'Man? I thought there were a number of them?'

Adams nodded.

'At the beginning, yes. There were a lot of them searching the river yesterday. They camped for the night. But when we scouted the ground on the other side, we found only the tracks of one man. Billy-Jo seems to think the others went back to their camp and left the one to hunt your husband. At this stage, it's just a guess. If we could bring the girl round. . . .' He grinned and patted her shoulder encouragingly. 'It's a messy business, I know, but see what you can do for her.'

Once again she felt the small surge of pride in his reliance on her and was glad he had not seen her in her moments of fear and humiliation. She said simply:

'Give me ten minutes and then I'll get your supper ready.'

'Thanks. We could all use it, I think.' He stretched himself out on the sand, leaned his head on one of the saddles, lit a cigarette and lay staring up at the velvet sky in which the stars hung low as lanterns.

He too had his own pride and part of it was to preserve his credit for strength, experience and laconic wisdom, with this woman who was another man's wife. By all his reckoning, Lance Dillon was dead, but until he could prove it, he could not say it because the saying might open a proposition he was not yet ready to discuss, even with himself.

The rape of the child-wife puzzled him. It was out of character with what he knew of aboriginal custom. Infidelity was less important in tribal code than the preservation of public order and the saving of face for the husband. A girl of this age would probably be married to an old man. Sooner or later, a young one would be expected either to seduce her privately or abduct her and pay the penalty. In either case, the presumption was that the girl would be willing and reasonably co-operative. Most natives set great store on their virility and claimed that their wives were insatiable. Inside the tribe, rape was an uncommon crime because there was generally no need to resort to it.

There were other contradictions too. As a Territory policeman, he knew something of forensic medicine and more of the sexual habits of the primitives. He had seen more than one case of sadistic mutilation. But the girl lying on the sand did not fit into this category. She had simply fought with her attacker and then been battered into submission. Again the question arose, why? She had been alone. She had neither reputation nor honour to defend. The man must have been known to her. Why was she prepared to risk violence and death rather than satisfy him?

Then a new thought came to him, half-formed at first but growing quickly into shape and solidity. He got stiffly to his feet and walked over to watch Mary bathing the girl's face with a damp towel, while Billy-Jo still squatted on his heels staring into emptiness.

After a while her body began to be shaken with rigors, her eyelids fluttered and her head began to roll from side to side. A babbling, incoherent mutter issued from her swollen lips. Adams took the towel from Mary and handed it to Billy-Jo.

'Keep bathing her. If she makes any kind of sense, talk to her.'

The tracker nodded and bent over the girl, crooning softly in his tribal language. Adams took Mary's hand and walked her out of the firelight down to the edge of the river. She looked at him curiously:

'Why did you do that?'

'Just tactics, Mary. If she woke and saw you, she would be afraid. She would probably say nothing at all. Besides, Billy-Jo understands her language. He's the only one to handle her.'

'You really know your job, don't you, Neil?' Admiration coloured her voice.

'I know the country, Mary. I like my job . . . most of the time.'

'What do you mean by that?'

He made a small, eloquent gesture of deprecation.

'Nothing of importance. Except that the work is easier if you can do it without personal involvement.'

She turned to look at him sharply but he was staring down the dark reaches of the river.

'Meaning you're involved now?'

'In a way, yes.'

'D'you want to talk about it, Neil?'

'No. Not yet, anyway.'

As if on a common impulse, they turned and walked down the beach, hearing as they went the low babble of voices behind them. For the first time since they had met they seemed to be in harmony, thought and emotion pulsing slowly in a matching rhythm with their steps. Their silence came placid and inconsequent as their talk, while the low current of communication ran uninterrupted between them.

'Neil?'

'Yes, Mary?'

'The girl back there . . . the thing that happened to her . . . how can people – even primitive people – live such brutal lives?'

'The answer is, my dear, that they don't. They live differently, but not brutally. They love their children. They love their wives. They are tender to them, though they never kiss as we do. Walk through a camp and you'll see a man tending a sick woman, stroking her hair, fanning her with a leaf, crooning to her. The same man, on a long waterless trek, might have killed her newborn child. But the two acts are not incompatible. They belong in different categories, that's all. Survival comes first. Survival for the group. A suckling child might hold back the mother, drain her strength so that she could not bear her part as a member of the trek. The fellow who raped that girl is as much a criminal inside the tribe as he is to us. In many things our attitudes are common, in others they differ, because the circumstances of our lives are so different.'

'Lance used to try to tell me the same thing. I was never interested before.'

'You never had to be interested. Your husband was prepared to think for you.'

There was no malice in his tone. He was stating a simple fact, baldly.

'Do you think that was a mistake?'

'I'm a policeman, not a judge, Mary.'

They walked on until they came to a large flat rock that thrust itself out into the river. They sat on top of it; Adams lit cigarettes for both of them and they smoked a few moments, watching the eddies swirling around the base of the rock. After a long while she asked him, hesitantly:

'Neil, can you explain something to me?'

'Depends what it is,' he told her with rueful irony. 'There are lots of things I can't explain to myself just now. What's bothering you?'

'Myself . . . Lance, too. How does it happen? How can two people like us begin in love, live together for a few years and end . . . the way we are?'

'Just what is . . . "the way you are"?'

Her hands fluttered helplessly as if trying to pluck the answer out of the air.

'For Lance, I can only say that he loves me, that he's hurt and disappointed and beginning to resent me. For myself . . .' she flicked her cigarette-stub into the water and watched it float away into blackness. 'For myself . . . I'm shocked. Somewhere out there, Lance is lying, wounded or dead. I'm going through all the motions of a good and faithful wife, but deep down inside me I don't care.' Her voice rose to a sharp, hysterical pitch. 'Do you understand that? I don't care at all!'

'You've had a rough day,' said Neil Adams with cool good-humour. 'You're in no condition to care about anything. For that matter, neither am I.'

'Is that all you can say, Neil?'

'It's all I'm going to say, Mary.' He gave her a sardonic sidelong grin. 'Neither of wants to eat our indiscretions for breakfast. You're tired and so am I. Let's get back and start supper.'

When they reached the camp-fire they found the tracker squatting beside the coals, smoking placidly. The blackgirl had lapsed again into unconsciousness and a small mucous foam had formed at the corners of her mouth. Adams stood for a moment, looking at her, then shrugged and turned away to talk to Billy-Jo. Mary busied herself with the meal, listening all the while to the rapid, low-toned parley.

'Did you get anything out of her, Billy-Jo?'

The tracker nodded, his old eyes bright with triumph.

'Name Menyan, boss. Wife of Willinja, man of big magic. Man who beat her want her long-time.'

'Why didn't she take him?'

'Willinja pointim bone, singim dead. Send kadaitja men killim. Woman no want dead man.'

'Why did they point the bone?'

'Killum bull. Try killum white man. Blackfella want no trouble with you, boss.'

'What's the name of this fellow?'

'Mundaru, buffalo man.'

'So that's it!' Adams's face brightened as understanding dawned. Then abruptly it clouded again, as the full import of the situation struck him. 'They're all out there – kadaitja men, Mundaru, Dillon.'

The tracker shook his head and shot a swift significant glance at Mary. His voice dropped to a whisper.

'Dillon dead, boss.'

'Why do you say that?'

'Easy, boss. Blackfellow way. Make killing first, eat liver fat, make strong. Take woman after.'

Adams frowned, pondering this simple pragmatic logic of the dark people. It was easy to accept. It fitted perfectly, the cyclic psychology of the primitive. But there was a flaw in it, and the flaw was Dillon himself – the twentieth-century man, whose liberation from ancient codes had thrust him into an area of unpredictability.

A sudden sound cut across the path of his thoughts, a scraping and slithering, a long splash, and gurgle of water.

'Crocodile, boss!' said Billy-Jo, quickly.

But Adams already had the rifle in his hands and the bolt cocked, while he stared at the pool of shadow on the farther side of the river. Mary Dillon watched, admiring the swift, automatic reaction.

'Over there, boss, by driftwood.'

The tracker's sharp eyes had caught the sheen of moonlight on squamous skin.

'I've got him. He's a big fellow.'

Three seconds later, Adams fired, and the next instant the big saurian was thrashing and heaving in the water, his tail clouting the piled debris and sending it flying in all directions. After a while, the thrashing ceased, the crocodile rolled over, exposing the pale underbelly, and drifted into a backwater under the pandanus roots.

Without waiting to be told, Billy-Jo plunged into the shallows and began wading across the stream. Crocodile skins were worth money and since a policeman could not engage in private trade, this was the tracker's perquisite. Before he reached the backwater he halted, waist deep in the water and they saw him fish something out of it. Then he headed away from the dead beast and back to the pile of driftwood. They saw him tear it away with his hands, scrabble among the debris and then stand a long time probing in the dark recesses behind it.

Five minutes later, he was back at the camp-fire, sodden but triumphant, holding Lance Dillon's shirt and trousers and the long, serrated head of Mundaru's spear.

CHAPTER SEVEN

M ARY STARED at the tattered garments in horror; but Adams spread them on the sand and examined them with professional care. After a few moments, he gave a low whistle and a gleam of admiration showed in his pale eyes.

'Your husband's quite a man, Mary.'

'I – I don't understand.'

Item by item, he pieced out the deductions for her.

'We lost his tracks just here, remember? He must have crossed the river and hidden himself behind that driftwood over there. He was wounded in the shoulder . . .' Mary gave a small gasp of fear as he showed her the rent in Dillon's shirt, and the brown bloodstains around it. 'He got the spearhead out, and dropped it in the pool. He probably tore strips of the shirt to bandage himself. . . .'

'And then?' There was tension in her voice. 'What happened then? Why did he leave his clothes?'

Adams laid a restraining hand on her arm.

'Take it easy, Mary. Let's think it out in sequence. He would have reached the river in daylight, yesterday afternoon. He would be wounded and weak. He would know that he had no hope in open country by day. What did he do? Settled himself into this place and waited for darkness. We know the myalls looked for him. They didn't find him, so they slept on the river-bank and waited till sunrise. Lance probably made a break during the middle of the night.'

'But why without his clothes?'

Adams rubbed a reflective hand over his stubbled chin.

'I don't know. It puzzles me. What would you say, Billy-Jo?'

The tracker shrugged.

'Boss Dillon cut holes in bank. Climb up. Maybe clothes snag on roots. Maybe wet and heavy for sick man. I dunno. Anyway, big mistake.'

'Why?'

'Night-time, no clothes, fine. Daytime, hot sun, white man burn up, finish.'

Adams frowned. The thought had occurred to him, but he would have preferred to leave it unspoken.

'Maybe. Maybe he hoped to work his way down-stream and take to the river again. We'll know better when we try to pick up his tracks in the morning. At least we know two things – he was alive when he hit the river. He was alive when he left it.' He turned to Mary with a grin. 'Now, can we eat, please? I'm hungry.'

His casualness was disarming, even though she knew he was using it only as a gambit to gain thinking time. But that was his right and she was too tired to dispute it. She began ladling out the meal; tinned stew, thick slices of damper – the bushman's bread, pannikins of coffee laced with condensed milk. While they ate, Menyan stirred and muttered in delirium. Adams got up to force more water and whisky into her mouth and draw the blankets closer around her. He hoped she would last till daybreak. A death in the night would add the final macabre touch to the complex little drama – and Adams, a good policeman, had no taste for theatre.

When the meal was over, they washed the dishes in the river, spread out the blanket-rolls and lay back, heads pillowed on their saddles, smoking a last cigarette. Mary noticed that Adams chose the place between herself and Menyan and that he was lying without a blanket, on his ground-sheet. She offered him one of her own, but he refused it, smiling.

'I've slept colder than this. Hang on to it. You'll need it before morning.'

'Let's share it then.'

'Bundling's a risky pastime. I wouldn't trust myself.'

To which blunt answer she had no adequate reply, so she lay back against the smooth cool leather of the saddle and watched the smoke of her cigarette drift upward towards the pendant stars. After a while Adams said quietly:

'You're probably asking yourself why we're not doing anything about your husband at this moment. I'm asking myself the same question; but I don't see that there's anything we can do. There's a couple of square miles of swampland over there. The grass is higher than a man's head. We could blunder about all night and find nothing. We could cross and re-cross your husband's tracks a dozen times without seeing them. Besides, there's Mundaru and the kadaitja men – they'd scent us like dogs in the dark. . . .'

'You don't have to justify yourself to me, Neil. I trust you.'

'Thanks, Mary.'

Her face was shadowed, so that he could not read it, but when she spoke again, her voice was shaky.

'I – I've learnt a lot today. Don't judge me too harshly. I'm mixed up, lost. But I'm still trying to go through the right motions. It's the best I can do.'

'You're doing fine, Mary.' His voice was gruff but oddly gentle. 'Go to sleep now. Everything will look different in the morning. Good night.'

'Good night, Neil.'

He saw her roll over on her side, draw the blanket up around her shoulders and before his cigarette was finished the steady rhythm of her breathing told him she was asleep.

Now that he was free of the problem and the provocation of her presence, free too of the need for constant movement and action, he could begin to pick up the jig-saw pieces and try to fit them into a coherent pattern. . . .

Lance Dillon first. A dour, driving man, tackling a problem bigger than his expectations, gambling beyond his collateral. A man not built for sympathy, who would either tame his land or break himself – but who had not yet learnt the elementary lesson of taming a woman. This was the tally up till twelve hours ago.

Now. . . ? A man cool enough to take a twelve-inch barb out of his own body, quick-thinking enough

to find himself a lair in crocodile water, bold enough –
or fool enough – to pit himself naked against the naked
land and the naked primitives who lived in it. Where
was he now? Half-way home, down the river valley?
Impaled on a killer's spear, like a moth on a pin? Or
crouched out there in the swamp-flats, dumb with
weakness or terror? The betting was all in favour of
the last possibility.

If he were dead the kites would be circling over his
remains, but in the last hour of sunlight they had seen
no carrion birds. Alive then. . . . But how long could
he stay alive? And where could he hide from Mundaru? If he were thinking straight, the swamp was
still the best place. But leave him there till daybreak –
what would be his condition after twelve hours naked
in the sun, two nights of wounds and possible poison?

Let him survive that too. Then ask could he survive
the shock of financial ruin and the loss of his wife? Or
perhaps he had already faced them, and found them
both bearable. But if you, Neil Adams, had bundled
with his wife tonight could you face him alive – or,
worse, could you face him dead?

Leave him then, a moment, and think about his wife,
resentful, discontented, afraid – hungry too, perhaps –
yet with a core of honesty and courage that keeps her
going through the motions of loyalty if not of love.
She attracts you; galls you like a pebble in your shoe.
She is frank about her unhappiness – a common
symptom of the spring itch. But she is equally frank
in blaming herself for it – and how does that weigh in
the cynical balance of experience?

You've never asked more of a woman than a happy tumble in the hay and a good-bye without any tears. Why should you care what goes on behind the brooding eyes of this one? She offered you a blanket. Was she promising more? When you refused it, were you afraid of yourself, or of her? If Dillon is dead, will you want to take over his wife? Or do you want to see first what is the truth of her? When you find Dillon with his eyes pecked out – or babbling on the edge of the last delirium will you be brutal enough to stand and watch how she reacts?

An untimely thought, perhaps. An uncomfortable indication of what years of solitary living can make of a passionate man. Push this one away too. Turn a policeman's eye on the drama which is even now being played out on the grass-flats. There is a rapist-killer out there. By law he belongs to you and you must take him. If you fail and the kadaitja men kill him, you must visit vengeance on them and the tribe – even though you know this will be a legality and not justice.

That's where Dillon complicates the issue. A tribal rape, a tribal murder, you can treat at your own discretion. Your report can say as little or as much as you choose and few will be any the wiser. But with a white man murdered, it is a matter for Headquarters, for ministerial reports, for questions on the floor of Parliament. Your career is at stake. Are you prepared to jeopardise it for the sake of an abstract justice? Twenty-four hours ago life was very simple. But now there's a woman in it and you can't read this one from a book of rules. . . .

Suddenly, out of the darkness, he heard the cry of a whip-bird, twice repeated. He sat up, every sense alert. It was night-time and the bush-birds were roosting. The black tracker sat up too and Adams stepped over Mary's body to squat beside him.

Billy-Jo's dark eyes rolled in his head. He pointed out across the water.

'Kadaitja men, boss.'

Adams nodded.

'I wonder if they've found him yet?'

The tracker shook his head emphatically.

'Not yet. When find him, hear Tjuringa – bull-roarer.'

'But they know we're here. Will they still use it?'

'Sure, boss. Kadaitja magic stronger than white man. Tjuringa make spirit-song for death.'

'We'll move in when we hear it. We sleep in turns, an hour at a time. You sleep first. I'll wake you.'

'Good night, boss.'

He tipped his hat over his eyes, stretched himself under the blankets, and was asleep in two minutes.

The whip-bird called again, and this time it was answered by the squawk of a cockatoo and the honk of a swamp goose. The cockatoo cry seemed to be the closest of all – down-stream and near the river-bank. Adams picked up the rifle, loaded it and hugging the shadows, began to work his way down towards the ford where he and Billy-Jo had crossed the river earlier in the afternoon.

When he reached it, he stepped in, planting his feet delicately one before the other, so that no splash disturbed the whispered rhythm of the current. It took him ten minutes to cross, and when he reached the other side he wormed his way up the bank and squatted in the shelter of a big thorn bush. The bird-cries were on his left, more frequent now. The man making the cockatoo call was very near the river fringe.

Adams waited, his heart thumping, holding the rifle so that the barrel was covered by his arm, lest the glint of moonlight on the metal betray him to the hunter. Time passed with agonising slowness – five minutes, ten – then the kadaitja man came into view. He was a tall buck, daubed from forehead to knee with cere-monial patterns, between which the sweaty sheen of skin gleamed in the pale light. He moved with a swift, shuffling gait, favouring the right foot, and when he came closer Adams saw that his shins and his feet were covered with parrot feathers and kangaroo fur. In his right hand he carried three spears and a throwing-stick, in his left a short club, carved in totem patterns.

Adams was not a superstitious man. He had lived a long time in the outback. But the sight of the painted man woke in him the old atavistic terror of the un-known. Death had many faces and this was one of them. He held his breath as the kadaitja man came abreast of him and passed on, his feathered feet sound-less in the powdery dust. Twenty yards ahead he halted, at the sound of the whip-bird call. Then he turned aside, parted the tall grass stalks and disappeared. Adams waited a few moments longer, then eased him-self out of his cramped position and slid down the bank to the ford.

Half-way across it, he heard Mary's cry, a long hysterical scream of pure terror. Heedless now of the noise, he splashed through the last twenty yards of water and went running to her along the sand.

Mundaru, restless on the border of sleep, heard the scream, and the marrow clotted in his bones. He knew what it was: the spirit essence of Menyan, haunting the place where he had killed her, because there was no one to perform the ceremonies of singing her to rest. She would be looking for him now, eyeless in the night, ranging over the swamp. She would not be alone. The 'wingmalung' would be with her – the malignant ones who strike illness into the bodies of those who neglect their debts to the departed.

He was lost now, without recourse. He had heard the calls of the kadaitja men, but he had counted on time to find the white man before they came to kill him at sunrise. Now he knew that even this hope was gone. There was no escape from the dead, no remedy against the malice of the 'wingmalung' except the tribal magic and from this he was forever cut off.

The terror grew on him like a palsy. Death was all around him. But even against the terrors of the spirit world, the primal instinct of self-preservation asserted itself. Menyan's spirit voice had come from the river. The kadaitja men were at his back. But all of them were still a distance away. If he ran, he might gain a little time – even though everything he knew told him he could not escape them utterly.

He picked up his spears, and bending double, began to work cautiously through the grass, away from the river, away from the kadaitja men. His limbs were cramped, his belly knotted, his entrails full of water. He moved slowly and with great effort as though he were hauling against a heavy load. He knew what it meant. Magical influences were at work on him, draining his life fluid, dragging him back.

He fought against them savagely, and after a while they seemed to grow less, although he knew this was an illusion. They were still there, still potent.

Eastward the moon rose higher in the sky and its radiance filtered through the mesh of fibres, lighting up his course. But even this held no joy for Mundaru. Menyan was named for the moon. The moon was an eye spying out his movements, reading them back to the spirit essence and the 'wingamalung'.

He dropped to his knees and began to crawl, close to the ground, as Lance Dillon had done before him. He was a primitive without understanding of irony. He was doomed and beyond the temptation of triumph. But a faint hope sprang up inside him when, after an hour's progress, he found that he was crawling in a set of tracks made by another man – a man bleeding, vomiting sometimes and leaving scraps and snippets of himself on the razor-edges of the grass leaves.

Billy-Jo was piling a small mound of sand over the body of Menyan, the moon-girl. Neil Adams was sitting on a blanket, cradling Mary in his arms, soothing her like a child after a nightmare. Her shirt was stained with blood, her eyes stared, her whole body was shaken with rigors. The words tumbled out of her in disjointed narrative.

'. . . Asleep and dreaming . . . I seemed to hear a cry. When I woke up, she was lying across me . . . her face on mine. She . . . she must have died just at that moment. . . . It was terrible. . . .'

She clung to him, hiding her face against his breast as if to blot out the memory.

'Easy, girl . . . easy. It's over now.'

'Don't leave me again, Neil! Please don't leave me!'

'I won't.'

'. . . Billy-Jo was down by the river. I thought you'd both left me. . . . I screamed and . . .'

'I know . . . I know. Now forget it, like a good girl. Did you bring any clean clothes?'

'There's a shirt in my saddle-bag, but this cardigan's the only one I have.'

He laid her down on the blanket, found the shirt and then peeled off his own cardigan and handed it to her.

'Get out of those things. I'll rinse them in the river.'

But when she tried to take them off her hands would not obey and her fingers fumbled helplessly at the fastenings. Adams knelt beside her and undressed her to the waist. She shivered as the cold air struck her and he drew her white body against him for warmth, while he buttoned on the clean shirt and drew the heavy cardigan over her head. She surrendered herself like a child to the small intimate service, and Adams was glad of the dark that hid his own face from her. If love were anything but a fiction of the marriage-brokers, he was close to it now in this rare moment of tenderness and pity.

Billy-Jo came ambling back from the crude obsequies and Adams tossed him the bloodstained clothes to wash. He tried to get Mary to lie down and sleep again, but she held to him desperately, and after a while he lay down beside her on the blanket, with her head pillowed on his arm and her arm flung twitching across his chest. He stroked her hair, and talked to her: soft tales of the island men, from Macassar and Koepang, who traded along the coast in the old days, quaint ribaldries from the miners' camps and the bullock-trains, legends of the dream-people.

Little by little the panic drained out of her, her body relaxed, her breathing settled into the easy rhythm of sleep. For a long time he lay wakeful, her hair brushing his lips, her breast rising and falling against his own. Then, finally, the cold crept into his bones; he huddled against her for warmth and they bundled like lovers under the same blanket, while Billy-Jo paced the river-bank and listened for the bull-roarers and the song of death.

During the night the last wind dropped. Moonlight

lay placid on river and plain and the ramparts of the Stone Country. The glacial cold of the desert crept across the swamp-land.

The cold was a trial to the kadaitja men. They were accustomed to going naked, night and day, but at night they slept with fires at their bellies and their backs, with the camp dogs curled beside them and their women-folk lending them the warmth of their bodies. This night of solitary, hungry walking was a ritual pain, another symbol of the sacred character of their mission. They must endure it until the cycle had been completed with the death of Mundaru.

The moonlight and the still air were other symbols – proof that the magic of Willinja was working in their favour. When the moon was high the man with the whipbird voice called them together and they converged on him accurately, although he was hidden from their sight. When they were all assembled, he had them hoist him on their shoulders, so that he stood, dark and massive in the sky, like a man walking on a moonlit sea.

For a long time he stood there, the light playing on his daubed body, quartering the grassland with his sacred spear, scanning every quadrant with eyes made keener by the aura of power within which he moved.

The whole country was wrapped in a silver dream. The swamp was flat as ice; the tree-boles were grey sentinels against the sky-line; their foliage drooped motionless against the stars. The grass was an unbroken carpet from the river to the lagoon and away to the dark ridges.

No bird sang. No animal stirred. Only the frogs and the crickets made a mystic chorus, punctuated now and then by the distant howl of a dingo and the haunting cry of a mopoke. The kadaitja man waited and watched while his companions grunted and braced themselves under his feathered feet.

Finally he saw the thing he had been expecting. Half a mile away, the grass was stirring as if a little wind were running through it, or an animal were nosing its way through the undergrowth. But the kadaitja man knew that the animal was a man and that his name was Mundaru. He knew more – that the magic of Willinja was working and drawing the buffalo man towards a sacred place, where the Tjuringa stones were hidden in a deep cave at the roots of a bottle tree and where the painted poles stood weathering round the leaf-covered entrance.

Before he reached it, they would take him. And when the spirit snake had been planted in his body, they would drive him towards it, so that he would die in the shadow of the power he had flouted.

It was enough. It was time to go. They lowered him back into the pit of grasses, and he told them where they must walk and how quickly, to come up with Mundaru at the first light of the new sun.

Some time in the small hours of the morning, Lance Dillon woke, cramped, chattering and agonised, but lucid for the first time in many hours. The place in

which he found himself was strange to him. The
ground was hard and pebbly and dotted with small
tussocks of coarse grass. When he turned his head painfully from side to side, he could see the shapes of
stunted mulga trees, white and skeletal, under the
moon. Ahead lay a low, tufted ridge of limestone, at
whose foot was a thick clump of trees. When he tried
to look back to see how far he had travelled from the
grass-land a spasm of agony shot through his shoulder,
and he lay flat on the harsh ground trying to recover
himself.

He knew very well that the lucidity was only temporary, a trough in the wave-like pattern of the fever.
He must hold to it as long as he could. In the bleak
radiance of the moon he saw how far he had strayed
from the river and how his last hope of rescue had
dwindled to nothing. It surprised him that he was not
more afraid – that he was even relieved to be absolved
from further effort and agony. The most he need
do was dispose himself to die as comfortably as
possible.

Many times in the years of his maturity he had been
troubled by the question: 'What would I do if I were
to lose this and this – my hope, my ambition, my wife?
How would I react, if tomorrow a doctor told me I
had only six months, six weeks, a week to live?' Now,
in this brief interval of reason, the answers were plain
to him. The hardest thing to accept was the inevitability of pain and loss and death. Before one accepted
there were the haunted nights when one lay awake
thinking of money and overdrafts, and bank managers

and the wise faces of the bar-room prophets who knew all about bankruptcy except what it did to the innocent victim.

There were the bitter days when one was too proud to ask for a kiss or a word of understanding, the silent evenings when a man and a woman sat together in a room, yet in heart a million miles apart. There were the hours when they lay a foot apart in bed, each waiting for the other to make the first gesture of reconciliation – and finally slide dumbly into sleep.

And when one day, the seed of death was planted in the body, there was the racking fight to dislodge it – the fight he had just endured and which had brought him to this place – waterless, barren, a hundred yards from the limestone ridges. One had to submit in the end, but once the submission was made there was calm, the calm of the silver age, the last quiet time before the lights flickered out altogether.

One more effort was demanded of him – to drag himself the final hundred yards into the shadow of the trees. Once there, he could compose himself decently in the shade and wait for death.

He raised his head again and sighted on his target a large bottle tree whose bloated trunk stood out from all the others in the clump. This would be his lodestar, the last goal of the last journey in the life of Lance Dillon. Summoning all his strength, he began to drag himself over the shaly ground towards it.

Every few yards he had to stop and rest, feeling the fever-wave rising to extinguish the fire of reason. He would lie flattened from face to foot on the pebbles, weak, gasping and waiting for the mists of weakness to subside; then he would go on, heedless of the sharp stones that raked his belly and his chest into running wounds. Each time he moved, he took a new sight on the bottle tree, and as he came closer he saw, ranged in a semi-circle before it, painted poles, some flattened like palm-leaves, some tall as maypoles, others hollow and thick as a small tree. Between them the ground was piled thick with fallen leaves.

Dillon had seen the like of them before many times. They indicated a sacred place: sometimes a burial-ground where the dead were stored in hollow palm-trunks, after their flesh had rotted away on platforms in the bush, sometimes a repository of sacred objects. The sight of it reminded him of the myalls who were coming to kill him. It was a casual reminder, tinged with irony. It was well that they should approach him with respect, walking over holy ground. Perhaps the ground might be too holy and they would fear to come to him – but he would still die and they could squat and watch him, just outside the painted poles.

His last halt was only five yards from the edge of the ring. The bottle tree lay perhaps another five beyond it and the intervening space was a carpet of dry leaves. He wanted to reach the tree, because its knotted, bulbous trunk would give him a back-rest, and he had the idea that he wanted to sit upright to watch the dawn and the coming of his killers. A bush-man's caution told him that the carpet of leaves might well hide venomous snakes, but a second reflection urged him forward. A snake-bite might finish him quickly – truncate the final agony to a manageable limit.

He crawled foot by foot over the last rough ground and into the dead leaves. There was a kind of pleasure in their touch on his scarred and naked skin. There was a dusty aromatic scent about them, as if an essence of life still lingered. He wondered whether anything of himself would linger after the final dissolution.

The tree was only ten feet away now, and he was pushing towards it through leaves as deep as his face, when without warning, the ground gave way beneath him and he felt himself rolling over and over into blackness.

Mary Dillon woke to moonlight on her face and the warmth of Adams's body against her own. His breathing was deep and regular, and under the rough texture of his shirt she could hear the strong beating of his heart. Her head was still pillowed on his arm and she felt the stubble of his cheek on her forehead, just below the hairline. His free arm lay slack over her body and the dead weight of it held her to him like a bond.

The last mist of sleep still clung to her and she surrendered herself to the comfort of his presence. She had slept three years in the marriage bed with Lance Dillon, but it was longer than she cared to remember since they had lain like this, relaxed, content, with passion a whisper away, yet dormant and unprovoked.

It was a sour comedy that a day's ride and ten minutes of terror had brought her to this point with Neil Adams, while three years of contract and companionship with her husband had taken her a lifetime away from it.

Whose fault was it – Lance's or her own? Whose fault was this moment of dangerous propinquity, when she shared the same blanket with a man who was not her husband. The love with which she had entered marriage had worn perilously thin under the chafing of time and circumstance. What drew her to Neil Adams was of new strong growth, hard still to define by name, harder still to deny, untested. Both situations carried a measure of guilt, but a greater one of accident and inevitability. In both the same question cried for an answer: where did she go from here?

Neil Adams stirred, muttering in his sleep, and his arm fell away from her. Carefully, so as not to waken him, she eased herself up to a sitting position and looked about her. The moonlit river flowed placidly through the night, where the shadows broke, the sand and rock ledges lay silver to the sky, and fifty yards away Billy-Jo stood, a black sentinel staring across the river towards the hidden chorus of the bull-frogs.

As if for the first time she saw the other face of the hated land – not hostile, but passive, not harsh, but empty and hungry for the touch to transfigure it to fruitfulness. What she was seeing now was what Lance had seen, in one mutation or another, and what he had tried vainly to communicate to her. In the first flush of revelation, it seemed she could get up and walk alone through the vastness without fear of man or bird or beast.

Lance had urged it on her many times, telling her that there were no wild beasts in the Territory and that even the wild nomads lived in order and peace, so long as their beliefs and customs were respected.

Then hard on the heels of the flattering illusion came the realisation that hardly a mile away was being enacted a drama of pursuit and killing, in which her own husband was one of the victims. As if to emphasise the pathetic fallacy, from far to the west there came the long mourning howl of a dingo. From the east another answered, then another and another, until the night was filled with a dreary graveyard chant, rising and falling like wind in the vacant air.

She shivered and slid back under the blanket. At the same moment Neil Adams opened his eyes. Their faces brushed. His arms went round her and the wasteland howling was hushed by his first whispered words.

CHAPTER EIGHT

IT IS NOT GIVEN to every man to approve the interior of his own tomb before he occupies it, and Lance Dillon was vaguely grateful for the privilege. He saw it from the position he would finally occupy in it – flat on his back on the sandy floor with a cone of darkness above his head and a moonbeam slanting downward from the hole through which he had fallen.

The hole was high above him and he wondered, inconsequently, what he must have looked like, flailing through the air as he fell. Then, as his eyes grew accustomed to the dim twilight, he saw that he had rolled down a long sandy ramp on to the floor. Tentatively, he moved his limbs, his head and trunk. They were painful but articulating normally. He was whole in bone and still lucid – an uncommon triumph for a man lying in his own burial-vault.

The air about him was dry, warm and clean, but tinged with a faint fusty odour which he could not identify, until his straining eyes caught the outline of the bats hanging from the fretted limestone above him. One or two of them disturbed by his fall were dipping about in the darkness with faint mouse-like squeaking. They were odd timid creatures, well-made for this graveyard dozing, but they were harmless and infinitely better company than the kites who would have come wheeling about him at the first warmth of dawn above ground.

He closed his eyes and let his fingers scrabble in the sand. It was fine and powdery, with no hint of moisture. Sluggish reason told him the rest of the story. He had stumbled into a cave, scored out by one of the underground rivers that had run centuries ago, beneath the surface of the Stone Country. Beyond this cave would be others, large or small, linked by a tunnel which was the course of the ancient river. If he wanted a deeper grave, it was here waiting for him, given the strength and the drive to find it.

But for the present he was content. The sand was soft. The warmth was grateful after the bitter cold above ground, and after the moonlight there would be the sun, striking through the peep-hole of the vault. He might not be alive to see it, but it was pleasant to think of, a hope to hold, while reason remained with him.

Slowly the vague shapes of his surroundings solidified; the groining of the rock roof, the pendant points of stalactites, the narrowing gullet of darkness where a tunnel ran downward into the bowels of the earth, the niches in the walls, stacked with stones, and bundles wrapped in tree bark. These last he could not identify, but he guessed that they were the weapons and bones of long-dead warriors cached by the myalls in their sacred place.

He wondered whether they would accord him the same privilege after they had killed him – whether even this primitive decency would be denied him. Not that it mattered. Not that anything mattered now, except a comfortable exit from the ruins of his life.

He had never had any religious faith. Philosophy was a scholastic mystery to him. His whole life had been dominated by the pragmatic cycle of birth, increase, acquisition and death. A man's only survival was in his offspring, and he was lucky if he died before they disappointed him. Death was the ultimate fear, but once one passed beyond this fear, there was only the calm disappointment that life had meant so little.

Suddenly the arid stillness of the air was broken by a sound; a single clear note, as if someone had flipped a finger-nail against a crystal goblet. The overtones hung a moment in the conical cave and then died. For a full minute Dillon lay listening, but the sound was not repeated. His thoughts drifted away from it.

. . . The drover's son who wanted to be a cattle king. . . . The snot-nosed boy holding a stirrup-leather for the great Kidman himself and gaping in wonder at the gold half-sovereign tossed for him to catch. . . . The stripling stock-rider, plugging his first thousand head of beef over five hundred miles of drought-stricken country to the rail-head. . . . The leather-faced gunner in the Japanese war, trading his cigarette and beer ration for a few extra pounds in his pay-book. . . . Keeping away from the girls on leave, because a night on the town was half the price of a yearling heifer. . . . The day his number came up in the repatriation ballot for a lease of Crown Land in the Territory. . . . The tent in the middle of nowhere, while his stock grazed on the river flats. . . . All the years of sweating and penny-pinching and denial, of meagre cheques and lean credit, until he could build his first house and pay off his first mortgage and make his first trip to the east to buy decent stock. So long as he was small and struggling, dealing in scrub bullocks and stringy beef, the big combines were prepared to leave him alone. . . . But from the day he made his first leap into the breeding business, they began to put pressure on him – always on the same tender spot: credit. When he married and began to build a household and a staff, the pressure increased, but the greater the pressure the tougher he became, the more determined and single-minded, so that in the end his whole hope of life, security and happiness became centred in the genitals of a bull.

Looking at it now, in the thin twilight of his burial-place, he saw it as a monstrous folly, next door to madness. Yet it was the truth. Other men had laughed and kissed and got drunk and bred sons they couldn't afford and laid their last shillings on a filly hammering down the straight; while he had lived, disciplined as a monk, in the service of a sacred animal. Who now was in profit – he or they? Who would be mourned longer, with more of love and pity?

As if to punctuate the unanswerable question, the tiny musical note sounded again. He strained at the tenuous echoes, but the next moment they were gone, while his mind still groped for the tag of association. . . . Sunday dinner at the homestead. . . . The meal all but over. . . . Two people with nothing fresh to say to each other, idling over the coffee and the last of the wine. Mary tapping absently at the rim of her wine-glass with a coffee-spoon, so that the heavy air was filled with the thin, repetitive note. His own voice, sharp and surprisingly loud:

'For God's sake, Mary! Must you do that?'

And then Mary's wintry, sidelong smile:

'Wears you down, doesn't it?'

'Why do it then?'

'Cattle for breakfast, cattle for lunch, cattle for dinner, cattle in bed.'

With each repetition, the spoon tinkled on the glass.

'That wears me down, Lance. I'm a woman, not a breeding cow. Don't you see what's happening to us? I want a husband, not a studmaster.'

'For God's sake, Mary! Be a little patient! I've told you a dozen times, we're battling now; but it won't be for long. A couple more years and . . .'

'And we're building bigger herds and better ones – while love gets smaller and smaller; while our marriage goes from bad to worse.'

'I've always thought it was a pretty good marriage.'

'You've hardly thought about it at all. And I'm beginning to lose interest!'

'You don't damn well know what you want. . . .'

And so on and on, through the dreary dialogue of disillusion, with its meaningless accusation and its hidden rancours that each was too proud to put into words. . . .

Now, when there was no pride left, it was already

too late. When he was ready to speak the truth, his swollen lips could not frame the words – and there was no one to hear them if he did.

Again the solitary crystalline sound rang through the vault. This time he understood what it was: the fall of a single drop of water into a pool. Behind his matted eyelids a picture formed: the slow seepage of minuscule droplets through the earth; their agglomeration at the root of a rusted stalactite; their slow, trickling course down the spear of limestone; the moment of suspension at the point; the final plunge into a basin where a million other drops had gathered safe from the sun and the thirst of man and beast.

Water . . . ! The last demand of the dying on a world of such varied richness. He waited until the sound came again and fixed its direction in his mind. Then he rolled himself over on his belly and began to drag himself towards it, hoping desperately that he would not find it beyond his reach.

Finally his hands touched the base of the wall and felt it swell into a kind of pillar above him. The next sound of water seemed to come from directly above his head. The problem was to raise himself to reach it. He drew his trunk and feet as close as possible to the pillar of limestone and then grasping the nearest projection, he began to haul himself upward, dragging with his hands, thrusting with his feet, holding himself by friction to the rough surface when each instalment of strength gave out.

Then the pillar broke off and his fingers clung to a

ledge. With a last convulsive effort he reached it and threw the upper part of his body across it so that he hung by his torso, with his face dipping into a shallow basin of icy water. The touch of it was like knife-blades on his torn skin, but he lapped at it greedily and felt it burning his gullet as he swallowed. Even when he had drunk his fill he still hung there, waiting for the little infusion of strength to seep outwards to his members.

His fingers explored the ledge around the basin and found it wider than their compass – wide enough perhaps for a man to lie within reach of the water. They found other things too: knobs and shards of limestone fallen from the roof, stalactites, long as daggers and almost as sharp. His fingers brushed some of them into the water, but closed on one, long as a man's forearm, thin and smooth and pointed like an awl.

Again the cool reminder that he was not to be allowed to die in peace; that the last moment would be one of violence and terror. He had not cared before. But now, in this quiet place, a coal of anger began to glow inside him. He had suffered enough. He had run to the edge of the last dark leap. Why should he wait tamely till they thrust him over it? His fingers crisped round the smooth butt of the stalactite, then slowly relaxed.

First he must haul himself on to the ledge near the water. Here he could lie, husbanding his residue of strength, cooling himself when the fever rose again. From here he could make the final despairing leap at the first of his attackers, the stone dagger in his hand, all the anger, disillusion and regret arming him for the hopeless fight.

It was the last hour of the dark when Neil Adams got up, settled the blanket around Mary and walked down to the river-bank to take over the watch from Billy-Jo.

The black-tracker had nothing to report. The kadaitja men had been silent a long time. They would probably remain so until the first light of day. He shambled up the beach, threw himself down on his blanket and curled into sleep like a bush creature.

Neil Adams sat down on a rock ledge, lit a cigarette and let his mind drift with the smoke spirals, while his body relaxed into the sad sweet contentment that follows after the act of love.

He had known many women, but this was the first with whom possession had seemed more like a surrender than a conquest. The ramparts of egotism had been tumbled down, the barricades of the Book of Rules had been taken without a fight. The legend of impregnability was destroyed for ever. He was a man who had taken another's wife, a policeman who had betrayed his trust and was open to attainder by any man who cared to dig deep enough into his secrets.

It was a bitter dreg to poison the after-taste of love, but it was there, and gag as he might he had to swallow it. Get it down then at one wry gulp. Adultery and professional dereliction. It is done. There is no way to mend it – and perhaps, after all, there is no need. The odds are all on Dillon's death, and what's the harm in a tumble with a new and willing widow? If he's alive, he doesn't know; and who's to tell or care – unless my lady has an unlikely attack of remorse? . . .

Even as he thought it, he knew it for a cynic's defence, harder to sustain than the simple truth. For the first time in his life he had come close to love – the pain and the power and the mystery of it. Mary Dillon had come to it too; and even without the consummation, the love would still be there – the pain too, and the haunting questions: Will it look the same when the sun comes up? And if it does, what's to do about it?

He stared across the water at the driftwood pile behind which Lance Dillon had hidden only twenty-four hours ago. Again he was touched with reluctant admiration for the endurance and resource of the man, naked, wounded and alone, pitting himself against the primitive to whom the bush was an open thoroughfare. How long had he lasted? How had he died? Had he known beforehand that his wife was lost to him? Did he end hating her or regretting his own failure to hold her? What would he have done in Neil Adams's shoes? Fruitless questions all of them – except one: Where was Dillon now? If anyone knew the answer, it was Mundaru, the buffalo man, and he was coming nearer to death with every minute that ticked away towards the dawn.

Neil Adams listened to the night, waiting for the

calls of the kadaitja men. None came. If Billy-Jo was right, none would come until the death-chant began and the banshee howling of the bull-roarer. He tossed his cigarette into the river and watched the current whirl it away into darkness. All his other loves had been like that – a swift enjoyment, a swift extinction. But who could tell how long this one might last and what fires might blaze up from its still warm embers?

At the sound of a footfall in the sand he turned sharply to find Mary standing over him, her face pale but smiling in the moonlight. He stood up, took her in his arms and they held to each other for a long quiet moment of renewal. Then they sat down together on the flat rock, hands locked but faces averted from each other, lapped in the tenuous content of new lovers.

'Neil?' Her voice was soft and solicitous.

'Yes, Mary?'

'There's something I want to tell you.'

'Go ahead.'

'Remember the old gag: "The hardest thing about love-making is knowing what to say afterwards"?'

He turned at the hint of mockery in her voice, but there was no mockery in her eyes, only a smiling tenderness. He grinned and nodded.

'I remember it. Is that your problem?'

'No.' The denial was emphatic. 'And if it's yours, Neil, forget it. There's nothing to say and nothing to pay. I'm glad it happened and I'll always remember. But if you don't want to remember, I'll never remind you. That's all, darling.'

'Is it?'

'From me, yes.'

'Is that a dismissal?'

Her face clouded. She shook her head slowly.

'It's an act of love, Neil. It's the only way I can tell you that you're as free now as – as you were with any of the others.'

'I may not want to be, Mary.'

'Then you're free until you find out.'

'And then?'

'Then perhaps I'll be sure too.'

He gripped her arms brutally and slewed her round to face him. His eyes and mouth were hard.

'Understand something, Mary! This isn't a bush meeting where you can back 'em both ways and hedge your bets on the outsider!'

'You think that's what I'm trying to do?'

'Yes.'

Her head went up proudly and she challenged him.

'All right, Neil! Here it is. What happened tonight was real for me. I wouldn't take back any of it, even if I could. If Lance is dead, I'm free. If he's alive and well, I was going to leave him, anyway. . . . And I love you, Neil. Now, what do *you* want to do about it?'

His grip on her arms relaxed. His eyes dropped away from hers. His voice lost its harsh commanding note.

'I – I think we should both wait and see.'

'That's all I was trying to say, Neil,' she told him coolly. 'I love you enough to leave you free. But don't ever tell me I'm hedging my bets. I did once, but never again.'

'I'm sorry, Mary.'

'I don't blame you. But I can't let you blame me, either. If I blame myself it's a private business, and I'll never ask you to carry the load of it. Now kiss me, darling – and let's not talk any more.'

But even in the kiss there was still the sour taste of regret, the comfortless revelation that guilt is a lonely burden – and that a man needs a special kind of courage to carry it in silence. Mary Dillon had it, but he wished he were half as sure of himself.

When the grey of the false dawn crept into the eastern sky, Mundaru the buffalo man halted, just inside the fringe of the grass-lands. He was cold, weary, hungry, and above all confused. All night long he had been creeping in the tracks of the white man. At every moment he had expected to come up with him, living or dead: but still he had not found him.

Ten paces ahead the grass-land faded out into tussocks and stunted mulga trees, a wide waterless area limited by the limestone ridge where painted poles were grouped around the sacred bottle tree. The whole space was empty of life or movement. The white man had disappeared and Mundaru lapsed into the final despairing conviction that he had died long since and that what he had followed was a spirit-shape, luring him to destruction.

With the conviction came a kind of calm. Death was already lodged in his carcase. He could hope no more, run no further. When the kadaitja men came, as soon they must, they would find him waiting for them, a passive participant in the ritual of propitiation.

Stiffly he got to his feet and pushed through the grasses into the open space beyond. The light was spreading now, the stars receding to pin-points in the grey firmament. A little breeze was beginning to stir in the leaves of the mulga trees. The bull-frog chorus died slowly into silence and the first bird of the morning rose, a black sinister shape in the sky ahead of him. It was a kite, and soon there would be more of them, many more, wheeling above him, waiting for him to die.

Half-way to the ridge he halted, laid down his spears, unwrapped his fire-sticks and squatted down on the ground to coax a little flame into a handful of dry, spiny grass. It was a meaningless action. He had no food to cook. The fire would have no warmth in it. But the motion of twirling the stick between his palms, spinning its point against the hard wood of its mate, blowing the first spark into a tiny flame, required a concentration that took his mind from the men who were stalking him.

When he himself had worn the kadaitja boots, he had found his victim crouched like a frightened animal, vomiting on the ground. He did not care to die like that. He could not fight. There was no challenge to the sacred spears, but at least he could go through the last motions of manhood, with the first gift of the dream-people flowering into flame under his hands.

Eastward the sky brightened, blood-red, as the sun pushed upward towards the rim of the world. The point of the spinning stick ran hot against the hollow of hardwood and a thin whiff of smoke rose from the tuft of grass. Mundaru grunted with satisfaction and blew steadily to coax out the first spark. A long shadow fell across the ground in front of him, and he looked up to see six men, painted and motionless as rocks, standing in front of him. In their upraised arms they carried throwing-spears, and the long, barbed heads were pointed at his breast.

The fire-sticks fell from his hands. The smoke was extinguished. Mundaru's arms hung slack to the ground and his eyes searched the painted faces above him. Between the bars of yellow ochre, their eyes looked down at him, cold as granite.

Then from behind him the bull-roarer began, a thin howling, growing in volume and tone to a deep, drumming roar. The air was full of it. The ground vibrated to it. It hammered at his skull and crept into the hollows of his bones and filled his entrails like wind. It stuffed his ears and seared his eyeballs and choked his nose so that he could not breathe.

The kadaitja men watched and listened immobile, their spear-points ready. The roaring went on and on for nearly twenty minutes, then stopped abruptly. Blind, deaf and shivering in the silence, Mundaru waited. There was a sound like a rush of bird-wings at his back and he pitched forward with the sacred spear in his kidneys.

Long before the bull-roarer began, Billy-Jo had the horses saddled and the pack-pony loaded. Mary Dillon and Neil Adams were standing by the fire drinking pannikins of scalding coffee. The tension between them had eased and they talked gravely and companionably of the day ahead.

'I'd like you to understand my reasoning, Mary. It could be wrong, but it's the only logic I can see.'

'You can't ask more of yourself than that, Neil. Go ahead '

'Strictly speaking, I should forget about the myalls and concentrate on a search for your husband. The tribal blood-feud is secondary, I can deal with that any time. But the fact is, we could cast about all day and still find no trace of your husband. Billy-Jo's the best tracker in the Territory, but even he can't work miracles. You understand that?'

'Of course.'

'So I'm working on the assumption that your husband is dead. All the signs point that way. This is the third day, and we know he was quite badly wounded. The only man who can give us any information is the man who's been tracking him – Mundaru. The kadaitja men are after him, and they'll get him – sure as God.'

'How can he help you then?'

'In a kadaitja killing, the victim lives for some hours. That's the point of it. He dies by a magical power, not by a man's hand. If I can come up with him before he

152

dies, I may be able to get something out of him. But I can't promise. . . . If we fail there, then Billy-Jo and I will beat the swamp for the rest of the day.'

'Neil?' There was tenderness in her voice and a curious touch of pity. 'You're a good policeman. Believe it always.'

'I'm glad someone thinks so.' He bent and kissed her lightly, tossed the dregs of his coffee into the fire and turned away towards the horses, just as the first booming sound of the bull-roarers sounded across the swamp. The three of them froze: Billy-Jo in the act of tightening a girth, Adams in mid-stride, Mary with the tin mug half-way to her mouth. Even in the cold light of morning, the primitive terror held them strongly.

Billy-Jo cocked his head like a hound listening. He flung out his hand in an emphatic gesture.

'Over there, boss. Long way. Outside swamp.'

Adams nodded.

'We'll try to skirt the billabong. No point trying to hack our way through.' He turned to Mary. 'Before we go, Mary . . . you ride between Billy-Jo and me. No matter what happens, no matter what you see, keep your head. And do exactly as I tell you. Understand?'

'I understand.'

'Let's get moving.'

He hoisted her into the saddle and they moved off, Neil Adams in front, Mary behind him, with Billy-Jo last and leading the pack-pony. They splashed across the ford, struggled up the steep bank and began to work their way up-stream along the narrow strip of clear ground between the bushes and the grass-fringe.

They had gone perhaps a mile when the bull-roarer stopped. Neil Adams reined in and they waited while he stood in his stirrups and scanned the swamp-lands, stirring lightly under the morning breeze. After a couple of minutes he lowered himself into the saddle, dug his heels into the pony's flanks and set off at a canter with the others trailing behind him.

For the next mile Mary Dillon found herself moving in a kind of waking dream, conscious of all her surroundings yet absorbed in an inner contemplation. She felt everything, saw everything: the thrusting muscle of the pony, the twigs and branches that whipped at her, the wind rushing in her face, the new light spilling over the land and the sky, Neil Adams a galloping centaur ahead of her. Yet her thoughts were all bent backward: to the river-bank, to the homestead, to the swift passion that had driven her into the arms of Neil Adams, to the slow death of her love for Lance, to the one vaulting moment in which the world and her relationship to it had changed completely.

She had seen the change before, in other women; but she had never understood it until now. There was an alchemy in the act of union. The transmutation for better or for worse was terribly final. One emerged from it curiously free; yet free in a new country, the contours of which hid mysteries unguessed at in the time of wholeness or fidelity. It was the old drama of Eve and the Tree of Knowledge, when the world changed overnight at the first bite of a strange fruit.

She was a wife, but not the same wife. From a creditor in marriage she had become a debtor. Her rights in law had been forfeited. The wholeness of herself had been broken and parcelled out, valueless to one man, to the other worth only what he cared to pay for it.

How much would he pay? How much was his hesitation dictated by fear for himself, how little by concern for her? How much did she care whether he paid or not, provided she could still read love in his eyes and a respect, however reluctant? And Lance? Was it only because he was dead that she could still think of him with tenderness? If he was alive, could she still face him with dignity? Even the most merciless self-security told her that she could. Few marital contracts were breached without fault on both sides and the moralist's finger often pointed in the wrong direction.

Ahead of her Neil Adams reined in suddenly and her own horse reared up on its haunches, and it took all her strength to hold and steady him. Adams turned in his saddle and pointed out across the grass-land to where a thin column of brown smoke was rising into the sky.

'What do you make of it, Billy-Jo?'

The black-tracker called back:

'Kadaitja men, boss. Takeum man. Burnem spirit snake in back.'

Adams nodded and turned to Mary.

'This is it. Close in.'

She edged her mount close to him so that their stirrups were almost brushing.

'How far, Neil?'

'About half a mile. We'll take 'em through the grass.'

'I'm scared, Neil.'

His hand reached across and closed over her own. His voice was very gentle.

'Don't worry. We'll be together from here on.'

As they urged their horses through the high rank grasses, she wondered what meaning she should read into those eight simple words.

Mundaru the buffalo man was lying spread-eagled in the dust. The kadaitja men were squatting round him, holding his twitching body, while their leader extracted the spearhead from his back. Beside them, a small fire was burning, and in the centre of the fire lay a stone, elliptical in shape and flattened on both sides. As the coals built up around it, they brushed them carefully to one side so that the sacred object was always visible, like a heart absorbing heat from the fiery body that encased it.

When the spearhead was extracted, there was a small rush of blood, and the kadaitja man held the lips of the wound together while he rummaged in the small bark bag which Willinja had given into his hands. He brought out a small sliver of white quartz, about the length of a finger, and this he inserted deep in the wound, covering it with a plug of brown gum-resin. Mundaru twisted and heaved convulsively at this magical invasion of his body, but the kadaitja men held him down and forced his mouth into the dust so that he could not cry out.

The leader stood up and walked to the fire. Without a moment's hesitation, he plunged his hand into the coals and picked up the sacred stone. It was nearly white-hot, but he grasped it firmly. He felt no pain, and when he laid it over the wound in Mundaru's back, the flesh and the resin were instantly cauterised, while his own hand was unharmed. When the operation was over, he laid the stone on the ground, filled his mouth with water and squirted it with his lips on the stone to wash off any evil which might have clung to it from Mundaru's body. When it was cool he put it back in the bark bag and stood up. The others stood with him and looked down at Mundaru, jerking and groaning at their feet.

It was all but done. There remained only the death-walk. They hauled Mundaru to his feet and held him until they felt him steady, then they pushed him forward. At the first step, he collapsed, but they dragged him up again, set his face to the sacred place and prodded him forward with their spears. Miraculously he stayed on his feet and, one hand clamped to the torn muscles of his back, he began to shamble ahead. The kadaitja men followed, with pointing spears, measuring their pace to his.

A foot outside the circle of painted poles they laid hands on him again and held him, turning his head this way and that so that his glazed eyes might see the symbol of all the power he had outraged. Now for the first time he began to struggle. This was the final vision of death. No matter how long more he survived, this was the ultimate agony. But they had no pity for him. With one concerted heave, they tossed him forward into the leaves and watched the ground swallow him up.

The echoes of his last despairing scream were still in the air when the shot rang out, and they wheeled to face the riders pounding towards them over the plain.

The scream woke Lance Dillon out of a doze, filled with the phantasms of fever. He was lying on the edge near the pool, one arm dangling numb and helpless in the water, the other still grasping the pointed stalactite. When he opened his eyes, he saw at first only a formless blur of light; but as his vision cleared, he understood that it was the sunlight slanting down from the entrance to the cave.

It was morning then. He had lasted the night. He wondered whether he would see the noon. He eased himself carefully on the rock ledge, trying to work a semblance of life into his numbed arm. The effort brought him perilously close to the edge of the platform, and as his angle of sight shifted he was able to focus on the spot where the sunbeam struck the sandy floor of the cave.

Terror flooded through him like a purge. Crouched on all fours in the sunlight was the figure of a myall black. As he looked, the myall raised his head, and Dillon could see the bulging eyeballs and the mouth drawn back in a grin from the white teeth. Recognition was complete. This was the man who had wounded him in the valley, who had led the trackers through two nights and a day, and who had found him at last, cornered and ready for the kill.

The myall moved forward out of the sunbeam, and Dillon lost him for a moment, when his head drooped and his body melted into the darkness. He could still hear him breathing in short savage gasps as he moved closer to the low pillar of limestone. Any moment now he must stand up, and as soon as he did he must come leaping to haul him off his pedestal.

He must not die like this, trapped like a rat in a dark hole. Every nerve in his body was alive with the instinct of survival. His fingers tightened round the stone dagger and he could feel the remnants of his will gathering themselves like a spring inside him.

With a huge effort he forced himself up to his knees, slewed his body so that his legs dangled over the edge of the platform, and he was sitting more or less upright. The effort made him groan aloud; pieces of limestone, dislodged by his movement, splashed into the pool. When his dizziness had passed he wondered why the myall had not come for him. His heavy animal breathing was closer than ever.

Dillon blinked away the sweat that bleared his eyes and peered about the dark hollows of the cave, searching for his adversary. Then he saw him, a pace away from the foot of the platform, still on his knees and snuffling at the sand. A faint highlight outlined the shape of his shoulder muscles and the line of his dorsal bones.

It was now or never. If the myall lifted up his head, it was the end. Dillon's fingers crisped round the thick butt of the stalactite and, holding it forward in both hands, he plunged downward on to the body of the myall.

He felt the point of it dig deep into flesh, heard the sound as the limestone snapped under his weight, then darkness swept over him like a wave, tainted with the smell of death.

CHAPTER NINE

JUST OUTSIDE THE RANGE of a thrown spear, Neil Adams halted his little troop and sat, erect in the saddle, watching the painted men, drawn up in line across the entrance to the sacred place. They were tense and watchful. Their spears were notched to their throwing-sticks and a single untimely gesture would bring them running to outflank the riders and cut them down. He might hold them off with gunfire; but this would mean killing and in the code of the Territory policeman this was barbarism, a confession of failure, a destruction of twenty years' work in the management of the nomads.

He turned to Mary and said quietly:

'I'm going to talk to them with Billy-Jo. If there's trouble, don't hang around. Ride like hell for the river and get the stockboys. Understand?'

'Yes, Neil.'

'For the present, stay here. Don't move until the first spear is thrown.'

'Do you think . . . ?'

'Just do as you're told.'

'Yes, Neil.'

'Billy-Jo!'

'Yes, boss?'

'We'll go on foot.'

The tracker shrugged and dismounted. Neil Adams made an ostentatious gesture of shoving his rifle back into the saddle-bucket, then he too dismounted, and the two of them walked slowly towards the painted men, holding their hands wide from their bodies, palms upturned, to show that they came in peace and without weapons.

Mary Dillon watched, white-faced and fearful. The kadaitja men watched too, measuring their paces, the fingers tightening round the throwing-sticks, their muscles contracting for the throw. Twenty yards from the enclosure of poles Adams and the tracker halted, straddle-legged, arms outstretched. The hostility in front of them was like a wall. Adams moistened his dry lips and said to the tracker:

'Tell them we come in peace. Tell them we know what has been done to Mundaru and that we know what they do not – that he raped and killed the wife of Willinja. Tell them where the body is and that they should take it back to their camp.'

The tracker grunted assent, paused a moment collecting himself, then raised his husky voice in the manner of the tribal orator. It rang in the emptiness, now high and dramatic, now rolling in long, resonant periods. His gestures were ample and expressive, and as he spoke Adams saw the kadaitja men look at one another in doubt, felt their hostility relax a fraction.

When Billy-Jo had finished speaking, they muttered a while together, then one of them laid his spears on the ground and stepped forward into the open space and began to speak. Billy-Jo translated for Adams:

'Mundaru dead. Eaten by spirit snake. Leaveim in spirit place. Blackfella business. White man no touch.'

'Tell them we understand blackfella business. Tell them Boss Dillon is lost and we think Mundaru killed him. This makes it white man's business. I want to go down into the spirit place and talk with the spirit of Mundaru. If they try to stop me there will be trouble for them and the tribe. Say that we have done service to Willinja and that we tried to help his wife. He has a debt to us. They will earn his anger if they prevent him paying it.'

Billy-Jo took up the theme again, embellishing it with the symbols of the people, translating the pragmatic logic of the white man into the involved spirit-istic reasoning of the primitive. Adams knew enough of the language to understand that the tracker was drawing heavily on the personal credit of the police-man with the tribes. He was emphasing time and again that Adams had always paid his debts, that he had never infringed legal custom, that he had never spoken with the forked tongue of the liar, that he had defended the black against the predatory drifters, that his friend-ship was strong and his vengeance terrible.

The answer of the kadaitja man was clear and emphatic. He accepted all the claims of the police-man – but the life of Mundaru was forfeited to the spirits, and the white man must not enter the spirit place.

When the answer was translated to him in clattering pidgin, Adams found himself in a neat dilemma. The myalls knew that the white man tried to save the victims of tribal vengeance and bring them to trial in their own fashion. They knew, too, the unwritten law that their own secret places must be respected. Defiance of this law would destroy his credit and earn him nothing but a spear-thrust in the ribs. He decided to play for time.

'Ask them, Billy-Jo: do they know Mundaru killed the great bull? And do they know that he was hunting Boss Dillon to kill him also?'

The answer came back; yes, they knew.

'Do they know what happened to the white man?'

No. They did not know. But if he were dead this debt was paid by the death of Mundaru.

Adams took a deep breath. He was gambling now – with his own life, with Billy-Jo's, and possibly with Mary's.

'Then tell them this: I believe that Mundaru tracked the white man to this place and either drove him into the spirit cave, or killed him and hid his body there. If this is true, his spirit will not rest, but will haunt the place for ever and destroy the magic of the tribe. . . .' And he added in sardonic parenthesis: 'For God's sake, make it sound good!'

The tracker shot him a swift, dubious glance and spoke again. This time the myall's answer was less hostile, more bargaining.

'He say you not sure, boss. You go down, maybe come up with Boss Dillon, maybe not. But you no take Mundaru. Mundaru belong spirit snake.'

For all the danger of the situation, Neil Adams felt a flicker of sardonic amusement at the neat way they had trapped him. They wanted Mundaru at all costs. He understood why. They were the official executioners. They must report a successful killing – otherwise they themselves would fall under sanction. To get what he wanted, he had to wrench the law in their favour, but their spears were at his breast; he had no choice. He turned to Billy-Jo.

'Tell them I agree. Tell them to go and pick up the girl. I will leave Mundaru in the spirit cave. Give them a message from me to Willinja. I will see him at sunset.'

The message was relayed. The answer came back.

'They want to stay, boss. Watchim go down. Watchim come up.'

Adams's face clouded with dramatic anger.

'I have never spoken a lie. If they do not believe me, let them kill me now!'

Even as Billy-Jo was speaking, he advanced, ripping open his shirt and baring his breast to them. It was the kind of theatrical gesture the primitives understood: man asserting his maleness by boasting and provocation. Three feet from the kadaitja spokesman he halted, and they faced each other, the painted man, the policeman, their eyes locked, their faces stony with mutual defiance. Then the kadaitja man grunted assent and turned away, Adams did the same. He had won his point. There was no profit in making his adversary lose face.

The kadaitja men moved off, heading back to the grass-lands and the river. Adams and Billy-Jo walked back to the horses. Adams's hands were twitching as he climbed into the saddle and picked up the reins. Mary questioned him shakily:

'You looked so small and lonely out there. What was it all about?'

He shrugged and grinned at her.

'A piece of haggling. They didn't want me to go into the sacred place. I talked them into it – or rather Billy-Jo did.'

The black tracker chuckled huskily.

'Boss Adams big fool gambler, missus. Maybe win, maybe all get bellyful of spears.'

'Maybe.'

He dismissed the subject casually, but Mary's concern and admiration warmed him like whisky and restored a little of the confidence he had lost on the river-bank. As they cantered across the open ground towards the big bottle tree, she asked him gravely:

'You have nothing more to tell me, Neil?'

'About your husband? Nothing. All we know is that Mundaru is down in the cave. We saw them push him into it. The chances are he's still alive. We take it from there.'

'I was afraid for you, Neil. When I saw you walking out towards the spears, I – I thought, if anything happened to you, I couldn't bear it.'

He mocked her lightly.

'Wonderful what you can take when you have to.'

'Don't laugh about it, Neil.'

'I'm not laughing, Mary. Just reminding you that what happens from here on may not be pleasant.'

'I know. I've been thinking about it.'

A few yards from the painted poles they stopped. Adams dismounted and handed the reins of his pony to Billy-Jo. The blackfellow stared at him, puzzled. Adams answered his unspoken thought.

'First, I'm going in alone, Billy-Jo. The myalls will be watching to see what happens. I've got to keep the promise. If Mundaru's alive, I'll send you down to talk to him. Wait here with Mrs Dillon.'

He rummaged in the saddle-bag and brought out a flashlight cased in rubber. He tested and stepped towards the gaping hole in the leaves. Mary's voice stayed him.

'Please be careful, Neil.'

He grinned and waved a reassuring hand.

'It's just a cave, full of bones and bats. I'll be back in a few minutes.' He stood a moment, shining the torch down into the vault, then stepped down the ramp of sand and was lost to view. For one wild second, it seemed to Mary Dillon that he had gone down into a deep, private hell from which he would never come back.

Half-way down the ramp Adams halted, listening and probing the darkness with his torch. There was no sound but the rasp of a tiny runnel of sand cascading down from his boots. The air smelt dry and musty, but tinged with the acrid odour of blood and human exhalation. The moving fingers of light picked out the bats hanging from the vault, the cavities stuffed with sacred objects, the glittering fall of the stalactites.

Adams focused it on the floor and moved it in wide sweeping arcs as he stepped down the last slope. From the shadows there came the single musical note of dropping water, and when he swung the light towards the sound he saw the two bodies, one flattened on the sand, the other flung over it like a sack.

He gasped with the sudden shock and drew back, then edged his way carefully towards the prone figures. They were motionless, silent. When he knelt to examine them, he saw that the upper one was that of a white man. He reached out a tentative hand and rolled it on to its back. At the sight of it, he gagged and turned away, retching violently.

The face was a swollen mass, the eyes and nostrils puffed, the mouth frothy and distorted. One shoulder was a suppurating wound and the skin about it was streaked and swollen with infection. The whole trunk was scored with scratches, blistered raw from the sun and caked with dust and dried blood. The hands were joined under the diaphragm, and held a stump of limestone between their clenched fingers. One rib had caved in under the impact.

Adams switched the torchbeam to the body of the myall and saw the stalactite projecting from the small of his back, and near it the cauterised spear-wound. He reached out his hand and withdrew it sharply from the cold and rigid contact. He slanted the torchbeam upward and saw the rock-platform where Dillon had lain. The picture was brutally clear to him. Dillon cornered in his last refuge. The dying aborigine blundering about the cave. The last panic leap of the white man on to the body of his hunter. Now they were both dead, with all their problems solved – and a lot more than either of them had ever guessed.

A wave of relief washed over him, and when it passed he felt strangely elated. The slate was clean, the report could be written with truth and discretion. The obsequies could be arranged to spare Mary any of this grisly spectacle, and after a decent time they could begin to think about their own future.

Then the policeman's habit asserted itself once again and he bent to make a final examination of the bodies. He raised the myall's arm and felt for the pulse. There was none. The cold of death was already creeping into the members. He jerked out the stalactite and tossed it far into a corner of the cave. No point in complicating the report. Cause of death – spear wounds. A kadaitja killing. Period.

He turned away and bent to make a similar examination of Dillon. He prised open the puffed lids and saw the eyes rolled upward into the head. He put his ear to the broken rib-cage and listened. There was no sound of a heart-beat. But when he felt the pulse, his heart sank like a stone in a pool. It was still there, weak, thready and uncertain. But it was there. Lance Dillon was alive.

For the first time in his life he understood the meaning of murder. The motive, simple but monstrous. The compulsion, overwhelming in its urgency, to sweep away at one stroke an obstacle to happiness. The opportunity, complete and flawless. Leave Dillon alone for another few hours and he would most certainly die. He had only to go above ground, tell Mary and Billy-Jo that he found both men dead and then, to spare the widow the grisly sight of the body, head back to join the stockboys, who would later return to pick up the body and carry it back to the station for a post-mortem, whose finding would be inevitable: death from a spear-wound, infection and exposure.

For one horrible timeless moment the thought possessed him like a madness. He could do it. He wanted to do it. Immunity was guaranteed. Here in the naked country, Neil Adams was the law. His word was beyond question. He needed only the courage to turn his face away and walk into the sunlight.

The horror receded slowly and he stood there, sweating and trembling with Lance Dillon lying at his feet like a rag-doll, muddied from a playtime of children. Then, before the madness could take him again, he stooped, hoisted Dillon on to his shoulders like a sack of carrots and staggered up the steep incline into the day.

They covered Lance Dillon with blankets and laid him under the shade of the bottle tree. They bathed his face, forced water and whisky between his teeth, felt the thin trickle of life in him surge a moment, then ebb again. They did all these things with a fierce, wordless concentration as though the simplest exchange might shout their secrets to the sky.

Mary Dillon bent, tearless over her husband, sponging his lips, wiping the suppuration from his eyes, holding his head up to take the liquid from Adams's pannikin. After the first cry of shock at the sight of him she had relapsed into silence, but her face was ravaged by an inner struggle. Her cheeks were bleached of colour, the skin was drawn tightly over the cheek-bones, her lips were drained of blood. Her eyes were a staring confusion of pity, of revulsion, of pain, puzzlement and sheer physical horror. Yet she worked gently as a lover, competent as a nurse, over the wreckage of Lance Dillon.

Neil Adams stood a little apart, smoking a nervous cigarette and conferring in low tones with Billy-Jo. After a while he came back to her and said carefully:

'It's time we moved. Gilligan's coming back this morning. I want to make sure the strip's ready for him to land.'

Mary Dillon nodded and asked in a dead voice:

'How are we going to get Lance there?'

'We'll straddle him on the pack-pony and then let him lie forward. We'll pad him with blankets and tie him on. He'll be as comfortable that way as any other.'

'Will he last the distance?'

Adams made a small, helpless gesture.

'God knows, Mary. Down in the cave, I thought he was dead. I wouldn't say he was any better now. We'll have Gilligan radio to Ochre Bluffs and get the doctor to stand by. The hospital will have a bed ready for him. It's the best we can do.'

'I'd never have believed he had so much endurance.'

Her voice had the same flat toneless quality and her face was a white mask.

'We shouldn't waste too much time. Give him another sip of whisky and then we'll get moving.'

Her next words shocked him like a blow.

'If he dies, Neil, you mustn't blame yourself. You could have left him there in the cave and no one would have known – though I might have guessed. If I have to, I'll tell him that.'

It was another lesson in the complex logic of women. He was still trying to digest it when they crossed the river and came to the landing strip to lay out the message for Gilligan.

The aircraft made two low circuits before it hit the strip, bounced along the rough surface and taxied to a stop abreast of the little group clustered in the shade of the paper-barks. Gilligan cut the engine, climbed out and came towards them at a run. When he saw Lance Dillon lying under the blankets his eyes hardened and he gave a low whistle of surprise.

'The poor devil! Where did you find him?'

Adams jerked a thumb over his shoulder and answered crisply:

'Over the river. He's in bad shape. You'll have to fly him straight to Ochre Bluffs. Radio the doctor and the hospital. Spear-wounds, sunburn, massive infection and exposure. Mrs Dillon will go with you. Have them make a bed available for her as well. Call for me at Minardoo homestead first thing in the morning.'

Mary shot him a quick, troubled glance.

'Aren't you coming with us, Neil?'

He shook his head.

'No room, for one thing. Second, I've got to get over to the myalls' camp and investigate this kadaitja business. Then I've got to return your horses to the homestead. Besides, you need a doctor now, not a policeman. I'll see you at the Bluffs tomorrow.'

'Of course. I – I'm not thinking very clearly.'

Adams turned away to talk to Gilligan.

'Can you make him comfortable in that crate of yours?'

The pilot nodded.

'We can slide back one of the seats and lay him on the floor. It's only an hour's run if we push it. He won't be too uncomfortable.'

'Let's get moving then.'

The stockboys lifted Lance Dillon and carried him across to the aircraft. Gilligan climbed in to prepare a space for his passengers. Mary Dillon and Adams stood a little apart, watching. Adams said awkwardly:

'I'm not running away, Mary. I've still got to clean up this job. There'll be time for us to talk later.'

She did not look at him, but said quietly:

'I understand, Neil. It's better this way. And – and I need to be alone for a while.'

Gilligan stuck his head out of the cockpit and yelled:

'All ready? Lift him in!'

They hoisted the slack body, wrapped in the grey soiled blankets and settled it carefully inside the fuselage. The pilot stretched out his hand, helped Mary into the cockpit and closed the door. He gunned the engine, turned the plane and headed it back into the wind for the take-off.

173

When she looked out through the perspex window she could see Neil Adams talking to Billy-Jo and the stockmen. She waved to him, but he did not see her and before the wheels were off the red ground it seemed as if he had already forgotten her.

The Auster climbed steeply, banked and headed towards Ochre Bluffs. When it levelled off, Mary bent down to look at her husband, wedged against the wall of the fuselage, padded with packs and blankets against the bumping of the aircraft. His eyes were still closed, his puffed distorted face lolled slackly on his shoulder and when she felt his pulse, it was still a faint hesitant beat. She knelt down awkwardly and prised open his mouth to give him a few more drops of water and whisky. Some of the liquid spilt and ran down from his mouth. She wiped it away with the corner of her handkerchief, then eased herself back in the bucket seat behind the pilot.

Gilligan turned and shouted above the noise of the engine:

'How's he doing?'

She shrugged and spread her hands helplessly. Gilligan nodded in understanding and tried to encourage her.

'Sit tight and keep your fingers crossed. I'll make the best time I can.'

She was glad when he turned back to the controls and she could look out the window away from the accusing face at her feet. They had left the river and the grass-lands, and the naked country spread itself beneath them, an emptiness of red plains, sparse gnarled timber, sandstone ridges and dotted ant-hills like lilliputian mountains. Heat struck down from a bleached blue sky and rose from the hot earth in waves and whirlpools through which the little aircraft bucketed like a live thing.

A clammy sweat broke out on her forehead and she fought against air-sickness, bending her head down to her knees until the nausea passed. Now of all times, she could not afford another failure, another humiliation. Now, more than ever before, she needed a dignity to face the final act of the drama. After a few minutes the plane steadied itself, the faintness passed and she wiped her face and hands with a soiled handkerchief.

She had spoken the truth when she told Neil Adams that she needed to be alone. From the moment he had come, carrying Lance out of the cave, every gesture had seemed like an actor's mime, every word a shameful lie. The rush of tenderness and pity she had felt for Lance had been dammed back by the presence of the man with whom she had betrayed him. Everything had happened so quickly that it still wore an air of unreality, like a game played in front of an audience. A game of truth and consequences, in which the truth was only part-spoken and the consequences still beyond assessment.

Hung out in the bright emptiness between earth and sky, her senses dulled by the drone of the aircraft, she felt the numbness of shock slipping away and reason beginning to take hold again. Her husband was alive. She could still feel for him and with him. The feeling

175

was changed from what it once had been, diminished, confused with other feelings for another man; but it was still alive – a residue of love for what was left of a husband.

How long either would last was another matter. The first love had slow weathering and swift assault. The man had succumbed too, and even if he survived how much of him would be left – how much of the tough sinewy body, of the thrusting disciplined but myopic spirit?

And Neil Adams? He too had gone through the scene tongue-tied, jerky as a puppet. What was he thinking now? What did he hope or fear from the brief, passionate encounter under the stars? What private devils had he talked with down in the spirit cave? How would he greet her twenty-four hours from now?

There were so many questions – and the answer to all of them hung on the same slim filament by which Lance Dillon clung to life. She closed her eyes and let her head rest against the resonant hull of the aircraft, while the wide empty carpet of the land unrolled itself beneath her.

The land. . . ! This was one thing she knew with certainty. She would never be afraid of it again. She might loathe it or love it, live in it or leave it, but she would never be afraid. She had seen the worst of it – the pain, the blind cruelty, the blood drying into its dust. Yet she had heard its music, had slept under its stars, surrendered to its harsh enchantment in the act of love. It was her country now and she belonged to it; just as she belonged to each of two men, unknowing still whether to stay or go with either.

Willinja, the sorcerer, sat in the shadow of the pointed rock and watched the two horsemen take shape out of a mirage and head towards him across the flat plain. He was not afraid of them, but he would be glad when they had come and gone. There were days, and this was one of them, when the years were a weariness in his bones, and care of his people was like a stone on his shoulders. He wished he could shed them, as a snake sheds its skin, and sit in the sun like other old men and let his young wives feed him and keep him warm at night.

He could not do it yet, because so far there was no young man fit and ready to undergo the ritual death and assume the burden of his power and his knowledge. Perhaps there never would be. More and more of the young bucks were drifting away to the white man's towns, to the homesteads and to the prospectors' camps. Those who were left were too preoccupied with the daily problems of living to devote themselves to the long preparation. It had happened in other tribes, whose names were now lost to the land. First they had neglected the knowledge which was the key to their survival, then their skills had begun to fail, their women become less fruitful, the totem spirits more hostile. Then one day there were only old ones left, shrivelled women squatting in the sand, toothless ancients mumbling at lily roots because they could no longer eat the strong meat of the hunters.

In the two men ambling towards him Willinja saw both the symbol and the cause of the change. The black man become the servant of the white, aping his manners, his dress and customs, rejecting the old knowledge in favour of the new. The white man taking possession of the land, thinning out the game, setting up barriers, bringing new laws, new diseases, breeding slowly into the tribes, yet destroying them as he did so. Even now, today, the white policeman could impose a penalty that would bring the day of extinction two steps closer.

The kadaitja men had come back to report the death of Mundaru, the murder of Menyan, the encounter with Adamidji outside the spirit cave. They had told of their bargaining, tried to justify it; but Willinja had shrugged them away. The bargain meant nothing if the white man was not disposed to keep it. His eyes narrowed, peering out across the hot dancing air. If they were bringing back the body of Mundaru it was a bad sign. If not there was some hope of a favourable outcome. But the riders were still too far away to distinguish the bulky shapes on the back of the pack-pony.

The body of his wife, Menyan, was buried on the river-bank. They would leave her there, marking it perhaps with a strip of bark or a heap of stones. The casual burial was good enough for a woman, provided that she were sung to rest in the proper fashion. Even now, back in the camp, they were making the preparations: gathering every article she had worn or touched, piling them in a hole in the ground to be burned when the sun went down. If they were not burned, the 'wing-malungs' would cling to them and bring sickness to the tribe. Even the name of the dead woman could call them up and so no one spoke it any more – not even her husband, who was a man of power.

Willinja would not grieve for her. He was too old for anything but regret and he could soon buy himself another girl-wife. But he could still be angry and his anger was directed against the dead Mundaru, whose wanton folly had destroyed a breeding woman and brought the whole tribe in jeopardy. Justice had been done; the blood-price had been paid; but only Willinja understood that the consequence of crime was a continuing curse that no penance could ever totally remove.

The riders were closer now and Willinja relaxed a little when he saw that the pack-pony was loaded normally and that no body hung across its cruppers.

When they dismounted and came up to him he gave no sign that he had seen them but still sat, cross-legged, tracing patterns in the sand with the tip of his finger.

Neil Adams sat down in front of him and waited. Billy-Jo remained standing a pace to the left of Adams. It was perhaps three minutes before the sorcerer raised his head and looked at the policeman. It was longer still before they began to talk, but even though Billy-Jo acted as interpreter it was as if he were not there and they were talking in a common tongue of matters mutually understood.

'There has been a killing,' said Neil Adams, calmly. 'Mundaru, the Anaburu man.'

'And Menyan, my wife,' said Willinja. 'And the white man?'

'The white man is still alive. Though he may yet die.'

'I tried to prevent it.' The sorcerer traced a complicated pattern and then rubbed it out with the palm of his hand.

'You sent out the men in feather boots,' Adams told him bluntly. 'This is forbidden. You know that.'

'Would the white man be still alive if the spirit snake had not killed Mundaru?'

A thin smile twitched at the corners of Neil Adams's mouth.

'Would not all be alive if your bucks had not killed the bull?'

Willinja stared at him with brooding eyes.

'You say we are under white man's law. Is the white man here to hold my bucks in check? Is he here to protect my wife? He comes and goes, and when he is not here who is afraid of him? But they are always afraid of the kadaitja boots.'

The logic was as plain to Adams as to the man who uttered it. Black or white, no one would heed a law without sanctions. If you are not here to apply them, then we must apply our own! Adams nodded gravely, considering the proposition.

After a while he said:

'You are the man who talks with spirits, Willinja. You will answer me this question. Who killed Mundaru? The kadaitja men, or the spirit snake?'

'The spirit snake.'

'If it had been the kadaitja men you would understand that I must take them to Ochre Bluffs for punishment?'

'I would understand that.'

'But a spirit snake is different and I cannot touch such a one. So I believe what you tell me. . . .'

A faint gleam of approval brightened the old eyes of the sorcerer. This was a man who understood the subtleties of rule. This was one who gave ground when he must but whose spear was still sharp and well-barbed. He said gravely:

'Today, Mundaru is eaten by the spirit snake. Tonight, we sing the "wingmalung" out of . . . that girl. Tomorrow, the white man's cattle will be safe.'

'I am happy,' said Neil Adams.

But Willinja had already dismissed him and was tracing a new set of patterns in the warm sand.

As they remounted and rode towards the homestead, Adams felt a small, familiar glow of satisfaction creeping over him. He had done well with Willinja. He had conceded a point but kept a principle. He had maintained respect but allowed another man to keep face. He had lubricated a little the rasping contact between twentieth-century man and his stone-age brother. And though no one would ever thank him for it, it helped him to feel a whit more at ease with himself. So long as a man stuck to the job he knew, to situations that he could control, he would sleep soundly at night. One step outside them and he was in bother. A policeman's follies were public property. He lived in a glasshouse and the taxpayers liked to keep him there, because they paid his salary and because they wanted value for money, security for their families and no shady bargains under the office desk.

So far, in the argot of the cattle-country, Sergeant Neil Adams had been a clean-skin with no brands on his hide. But tomorrow, back at Ochre Bluffs, would he brand himself – lover to Lance Dillon's widow, or co-respondent in his divorce? By moonlight and star-shine it was easy to talk of love; but by daylight there were a dozen dirtier names, and the raw realists of the Territory knew them all.

As they rode he found himself turning to look at Billy-Jo and wondering how much the black tracker had seen on the river-bank, and how he had judged this unaccustomed commerce of Boss Adams.

All of a sudden he was sick of his own cynicism. He loved this woman. He had been tempted to murder to hold her. If love meant anything it meant honesty, courage, a high head and a clear eye and a challenge to the world to wreck it if it dared.

Why then was he skulking away – from Mary, away from himself, away from the cat-calls of a back-country bar?

Then at one stride he came up with the truth. It was not the love that was in question, hers or his. It was the cost – his own willingness to surrender the whole or a part of himself to any woman. To be a lover was one thing – all care taken and no responsibility. To be a husband was quite another – all care, all responsi-bility and the wedding-ring worn like a hobble-chain on a brumby stallion. It was pleasant to finger the price-tag, but to put the money on the counter, wrap up the goods and carry them away for better or for worse – eh! this was much, much different.

The ponies ambled homeward through the dust and the heat-haze, while Neil Adams lolled in his saddle and thought of Mary Dillon flying back to face, alone, the crisis he had precipitated for her.

CHAPTER TEN

LANCE DILLON was climbing out of a spiral pit of darkness. The climb was slow and painful, full of checks and reverses. Sometimes he fell dizzily into emptiness. Sometimes he groped against a solid handhold and felt on his eyeballs the weight of a light he could not see. Sometimes he was cold as death, sometimes burning in a black furnace.

The darkness in which he moved was alive. Batwings brushed his face, black hands reached out to hold him, spear-points pricked at him, water dripped in maddening monotony, the palpitant air lay over him like a blanket. There were voices too, talking without words, uttering words without sense. Some of the voices were strange, some vaguely familiar, like faces seen in a fog.

Even in this blind world there was a perspective, a sense of extension and relation. But the perspective was always changing – now rocketing away into infinity, now contracting on him like a concertina. The sounds swelled in wild climaxes then died into haunting cadences, elusive as whispers in a twilit street.

In the galactic darkness he seemed to have undergone a strange metamorphosis. The small core of himself was the same, but the rest of him, the conformation of trunk and limb and feature, seemed to have slipped out of mould and into fluidity. He might have been a snake in a hollow log, a wombat in a tunnel, a chrysalis in a cocoon, for all the certainty that was left.

For a long while the darkness was absolute, but then a light began to show, blurred and transient, always a long way beyond the reach of his groping fingers. Later it solidified, stayed a little longer, haunted him with its suggestion of an outline. By now he was higher in the pit, sensible of some faint progress – though towards what he could not tell. Then, at one moment in the timeless continuum, the light took form and he found himself looking into Mary's face. He tried to reach for her, but made no contact. He tried to call to her but no sound came, then her face melted into light and the light was snuffed back into blackness.

For a long time afterwards it seemed that he hung suspended near the peak of the spiral, a breath away from some kind of revelation. What it was he could not guess, nor even care greatly, being weary from the long climb out of nowhere. Finally, without knowing how, he drifted out of limbo and into sleep; and when he opened his eyes, he saw a man bending over him, a black-haired fellow with stubbled cheeks and a wide grin and a stethoscope dangling from his ears. Dillon was still fumbling drowsily for his name, when a raw cheerful voice said:

'So you're awake, eh? They breed 'em tough on Minardoo.'

It was the voice that jogged the wheels of memory into motion. Dillon tried to grin back but his lips were numb and his own voice issued in a husky squawk.

'Black Bellamy! the mad doctor! How am I doing, Doc?'

Doctor Robert Bellamy took the stethoscope out of his ears and hung it round his neck. He sat down on the edge of the bed, chuckling:

'By rights you should be dead. I've never seen such a bloody mess.'

Dillon struggled to sit up, but pain broke out over his body and he lay back, sweating, on the pillows. Bellamy cocked a cynical eye at him and grinned again.

'Let that be a lesson to you; take it slow and easy. You're burnt raw, back and front. You're full of formic acid, and there's still enough sepsis in that shoulder to kill a bullock. You're going to be with us a long time yet.'

Dillon blinked away the pain and asked thickly:

'How long have I been here?'

'This is the third day.'

'How did I get here?'

'Neil Adams found you. Your wife brought you in.'

'Mary. . . .' Just as he had come to the end of his groping, the darkness was clouding in on him again. 'Mary . . . where is she?'

'Resting. She's been with you night and day since you came. You're going to rest yourself now. Then you can talk to her.'

He felt the prick of a hypodermic in his arm, saw the dark stubbled face ballooning into a fog above him, then the blackness swallowed him up once again.

Doctor Robert Bellamy frowned and wiped the sweat

from his forehead with a khaki handkerchief. He had had a rough week, two hard deliveries, an outbreak of measles in the aborigine settlement, one punctured lung after a brawl in the bar and a smash on the Darwin road that added up to a crushed arm, a ruptured spleen and some quick, if unbeautiful, plastic surgery. And for the last three days Dillon had been fighting a drawn battle with death while they pumped penicillin into him and had Gilligan screaming up to Darwin for fresh supplies.

Now, it seemed Dillon had won his battle. But it was a partial victory at best. Every auscultation confirmed it. The human heart is the toughest organ in the body, but Lance Dillon's had taken one round of punishment too many. He would recover. He could lead a normal, temperate life. But his hard-driving days were over. He had ridden to his last muster, thrown his last steer. And Black Bellamy wondered how he would take the news.

He folded his stethoscope, shoved it into the pocket of his bush shirt and walked across the dusty little compound of the hospital to the grey iron-roofed bungalow that was the nurses' quarters. He pushed open the screen door and walked into the cool dim lounge with its rattan furniture, its piles of old fashion magazines and its pots of struggling cactus and trailing creeper. Mary Dillon swung her legs off the settee and stood up to greet him.

'Sit down, Doctor. I'll pour you a drink.'

She walked to the kerosene refrigerator in the corner and brought out a bottle of beer and two glasses. As she stood pouring for him and for herself, Bellamy watched her with hooded speculative eyes. In the last three days, she had grown visibly older – no, older wasn't the word; maturer, that was it. The skin was still young and unlined, the figure firm, the walk springy and confident. But the lines had hardened, somehow. The skin had tightened over the bones of her face, the mouth had thinned a little; the eyes looked into farther distances: there was an air of deliberation and control about her, as if she were walking a little strangely in a new estate.

She handed him his glass, carried her own to the settee and sat down. They toasted each other ritually and drank. She questioned him calmly.

'How is Lance?'

Bellamy took another long draught of beer and re-filled his glass before he answered:

'Pretty well, considering what he's been through. The infection's under control. The broken rib will mend in time. The burns are clearing up, slowly. We'll have him up and about in a few weeks.'

'Is that all?' She was watching him over the rim of her glass, her eyes, shadowed with weariness and want of sleep, probing him.

He hesitated a moment. Then shrugged and gave it to her bluntly.

'Not quite all. There's a certain amount of damage to the heart.'

'How much damage?'

'Well . . . we'd need more tests than I can make to establish it fully. But in general terms, he'll have to slow down. No heavy work, no violent exercise. A regular routine, as little anxiety as possible. On a careful regimen, he could outlast both of us.'

'Can he still run Minardoo?'

Bellamy shook his head.

'Not the way he's been doing it. With a good manager and a good foreman, maybe, yes. But I understand you've been having a rough time lately?'

'We've been short of money, yes.'

'And now you've lost the bull.'

'Yes.'

'That makes it very rough. I wouldn't like to see Lance going back to that.'

Her eyes were cool as ice.

'Any other suggestions, Doctor?'

He cocked his head on one side and spread his hands in a comical gesture of deprecation.

'Cut your losses. Get out. Get Lance a desk job with the pastoral company, handling other people's mortagages.'

'That would kill him quicker than anything.'

'It probably would at that.'

'Have you told Lance?'

'Not yet. I'd like to wait till he's stronger. It'll give you some time to think things out too.'

'I've already done that. We're going to carry on Minardoo. I'll run it myself until Lance is well. Then we'll share it.'

His bushy eyebrows went up in surprise, and she gave him a little ironic smile.

'You don't think I can do it?'

'I didn't say that. I've confined too many women not to know how tough they are.' He chuckled and buried his nose in his drink; then he quizzed her shrewdly. 'One small point – what will you use for money?'

'I called the pastoral company and asked for a new loan.'

'What did they say?'

'They refused – at first. Then I told them they could foreclose any day they wanted, provided they could get someone to work the place. And I'd plaster the story all over the country about how they put a returned serviceman off his land because the blacks had killed his bull and damn near killed him.'

'And they took it?'

'They took it and liked it, Doctor. They'll give us another three years and enough capital to see us through.'

For a moment he stared at her in amazement, then threw back his dark tousled head and laughed:

'For God's sake! That's the best damn story I've heard in years. But you . . . you of all people! The city chick chirping up to the crows and the bush-hawks. Lord love you, girl, I didn't think you had it in you! I remember the first night Lance brought you to a dance at Ochre Bluffs. I thought it and I said it: "Give her eighteen months and she'll be scuttling home to mother!"'

'A lot's happened since that night, Doctor.'

The tone of her voice, the chill appraising look in her eyes, choked off his laughter and reduced him to blushing embarrassment. He mumbled an apology, finished his beer with indecent haste and went out, wondering.

Strange things happened to the folk who lived in the naked country. What had happened to Mary Dillon in the three years of her marriage, in the five days of her search and vigil for her husband? And what would happen to the husband when the soft hands of the city girl took over the reins of the power?

Alone in the dim room, Mary Dillon poured the last of the beer into her glass and drank it slowly. She had behaved like a shrew and she knew it – regretted it too, because she had always felt a softness for Robert Bellamy, bush doctor, old Territory hand, and kindest of souls this side of the sunset. Yet she could not help herself. It was as if she had called up every last reserve – of pity, gentleness, courage – to bolster her decision to stay with Lance. Now there was nothing left, just the hard stone of resolve set where her heart had once been and no love or laughter or tenderness left to spend on anyone.

The feeling terrified her. It was as if she had signed her own death warrant – or vowed herself to a closed convent while the sap of youth still ran sweet. The future stretched before her, bleak as the Stone Country under a dry moon. Why had she done it? Not for the moralists with their pointing fingers. Not for guilt and penance. You can live with the guilt and there are twenty rougher substitutes for a hair-shirt. Why then?

She could answer it now, in the wintry calm of decision. . . . Because it takes a tougher woman than Mary Dillon to sit with a man – any man – for three days and two nights and watch him battling for breath, battling for life, to hear him call your name while the microbes are eating at his blood and the poison is clotting in his heart muscles, to hold his hand and feel it grip yours as if it were the life-strand, to watch death take hold of him and see him fight his way free – and then take your own table-knife and cut his throat. There's a whore in every woman, but there are things even a whore won't do for love or money. So you sit here, sipping your beer, a brave little woman taking on a man's job, bargaining with the bankers, bullying the stockmen, bolstering a husband old before his time and wondering what it will feel like when your womb dries up and the callouses grow on your hands and there's leather in your voice and the sour taste of disillusion on your tongue. . . .

She could answer it now and know that, right or wrong, it was the only answer for her. Lance might have a different one; Neil Adams too. But this was another lesson she had learned; you live with a man for breakfast and dinner and the Sunday roast. For eight hours of bedtime you love him or loathe him. But the only one you live with twenty-four hours of a day is yourself. And for so much of living you need so much of self-respect if you're not going to hit the bottle or run crazy with a meat-cleaver.

The glass was empty now. She put it down on the

table, lay back on the settee, closed her eyes and thought about Neil Adams.

She had seen him once and briefly on his return from Minardoo. He had come to the hospital and found her sitting at Lance's bedside, screened from the rest of the ward. He had made solicitous inquiries, he had held her hand for a few furtive moments. They had kissed, quickly, without passion. Then he had gone, too quickly, with too little regret. She did not blame him. It was too much to ask of the most devoted lover to enjoy an embrace at the husband's death-bed. But he had not come to her since, whether from decency or discretion – and there had been moments when heart and body cried out for the comfort of his arms. Had he urged differently she might have decided differently about her future with Lance; but he had not spoken and when the choice was made there was a kind of stale satisfaction in the thought that she wanted him still, but needed him not half so much.

Soon it would be her turn to go to him. But not yet. Not for a little while. Until the words were spoken, he belonged somewhat to her and she to him. She had earned the right to dream a space, hold a mite longer to the last illusion. The weariness of the long vigil crept in on her and she slept, dreaming of Neil Adams with the moon on his face and his arms reaching up to draw her lips to his.

In the fall of the afternoon, while the shadows of the

bluffs lengthened across the dusty town, Sergeant Neil Adams sat in his office writing the last pages of his report on Lance Dillon and the kadaitja killing. It was a neat piece of work and he was proud of it. The facts were laid out in order – all facts that headquarters needed to know – dates, times, places, the simple sequences of physical events. It leaned – but not too emphatically – on the action taken by the officer in charge. It lingered – but not too long – on the reasons for the action, the fortunate outcome, the preventive diplomacy which was a guarantee against further trouble with the tribes.

It would read well in Darwin. It would read better still in extract on the Minister's file in Canberra. And the memorandum scribbled on the margins would read best of all. 'Action approved. An efficient and far-sighted officer, with profound knowledge of the area and its indigenous peoples.' These things were important to an ambitious policeman. They would be read and noted and recalled when the names went into the hat for appointments and promotions.

It was equally important to know what to leave out. Many a good servant of the State had died in obscurity because he had a garrulous pen. Many a promising man had written his own epitaph when he lapsed from fact into speculation. Neil Adams had much to ponder in the case of Lance Dillon and his wife, but he was too canny to commit it to paper.

So he wrote on, slowly and thoughtfully, until a shadow fell across his desk and he looked up to see Mary Dillon standing over him, pale but composed, a little smile breaking on her lips. He cast a quick side-long glance at the window but there was no one to be seen, except Billy-Jo sitting by the veranda-post whittling a stick. He stood up and took Mary in his arms. Their lips brushed, and then, gently but firmly, she disengaged herself.

'Sit down, Neil.' Her voice was calm, but remote. 'I'd like to talk to you.'

He hesitated a moment, but she put her hands on his shoulders and pushed him back in his chair. Then she sat down opposite him, hands folded in her lap, her eyes fixed on his face. He said gently:

'It's nice to see you, Mary. I'm sorry we couldn't get together before; but it didn't seem wise. This is a small town. People talk.'

'I understand that.' There was no rancour in the level tone. 'But we had to talk sooner or later, didn't we?'

'Of course. How is your husband?'

'Doctor Bellamy says he's out of danger now.'

'I'm glad to hear it.'

'Are you, Neil?'

He had not expected to be cornered so quickly. He flushed and stammered. 'Well – you know what I mean. It's . . . it's the thing you say. . . .'

'What did you really mean, darling?'

'I'm glad for him – and sorry for us.'

'Why sorry, Neil? If we love each other, we can still arrange things – one way or another.'

'It's not as easy as that. Don't you see. . . ?'

His face was troubled. His eyes fell away from hers.

Her heart went out to him in his humiliation and perplexity but she still pressed him brutally.

'Neil, answer me one question. Do you love me?'

'You know I love you, Mary. But . . .'

He could not complete the sentence. The single word hung between them like a suspended chord of music – minor music lost and plaintive. She knew it was no use hurting him or hurting herself any more. Everything had been said. The rest was postscript and dispensable.

She stood up, took his face between her hands and kissed him full on the lips. There were tears in her eyes but her voice was steady.

'I love you, Neil. Not as much as I did. Not as much as I could. But wherever I am, whatever happens, there'll still be a corner of my heart that belongs to you. Goodbye, darling.'

She turned away and he sat like a stone man, watching her go. With her hand on the door-knob, she turned back:

'I almost forgot to tell you – I decided before I came – I'm staying with Lance. I'll be running Minardoo from now on.'

Before he had time to think, he was half-way out of his chair, and the words were on his lips:

'Are you going to – tell him about us?'

For a long moment she stared at him, shocked, silent and contemptuous, then she opened the door and walked out into the sunlight. Neil Adams sat down heavily at his desk, buried his face in his hands, and for the first time in his life found grace to be ashamed of himself.

Three days later, Lance Dillon lay behind white screens and wrestled with the black imps of despair. Bellamy had given him the verdict, calmly, precisely. Then, wise fellow that he was, had left him to digest it in privacy. His first reaction was to reject it utterly. He was getting stronger every day, healing as a healthy man should. A fellow was half-way into the grave when he could not sit a horse and plug round the herds and hold a yearling under the iron for a mere five seconds.

Then cold reason told him that Bellamy had no cause to lie. He knew better than any the loads a man had to carry, with the bankers yapping at his heels every step of the way. If Bellamy said it, it was true. If it were true, he was a cripple for life, and this was a cruel country for the halt and the maimed.

Then the whole hideous irony of it broke on him. He had survived so much – hunger, thirst, the spears of the black hunters, the terror of death in a dark place. Now he was reduced to this – a young-old man, nursing his heart in the shade, while herds wheeled under the whips and came thundering home through the paper-barks. It was too much for one man to take. Soft curses came bubbling out of his lips. Tears forced themselves out from his shut lids and trickled down the raw new skin of his cheeks.

Then Mary came in, an unfamiliar figure in jodhpurs and a starched shirt. Her hair wind-blown, her face tinged brown from the afternoon sun. She kissed him lightly on the forehead, wiped the tears from his cheeks and sat down beside the bed. She said gently:

'So Bellamy told you?'

'Yes. . . .' He caught at her hands and his voice broke in desperate appeal. 'I can't take it, Mary. It's too much. I can't . . . I can't . . .!'

'Listen to me, Lance!' The command in her voice checked him abruptly. He stared at her, puzzled, vaguely afraid. 'You're going to take it: because it isn't half as bad as it looks. When you're out of here, we're going back to Minardoo. We're going to run it together.'

'Together?' The word seemed unfamiliar to him. 'You – you don't know anything about the cattle business, and besides, we're broke . . . flat broke.'

For the first time she smiled at him, an odd, secret smile.

'No, Lance. We're in business. I've got us a three-year extension and some extra working capital to get us going again. You know where I've been this afternoon? Down at the stockyards watching an auction.'

'My God, Mary!' Panic made him seem for a moment like his old self. 'You didn't buy anything?'

'No.' She patted his hand in maternal assurance. 'But I learned a lot. I'll learn more and quicker as time goes on. . . . If you want me to, that is.'

He stared at her, unbelieving.

'You . . . you've changed, Mary. I don't know how, but you've changed.'

Her face clouded. The sparkle went out of her voice. She nodded slowly.

'Yes, Lance. I've changed. I'm going to tell you how and why. I want you to listen. Afterwards, you will tell me what you want to do.'

'I don't understand.' He frowned, searching her face with troubled eyes.

'I'm going to try to make you understand. Before all this happened, I was going to leave you.'

'Leave me?' It was a high note of panic. 'You mean for good?'

'Yes.'

He closed his eyes and grappled with the thought. When he opened them again, she saw that he understood. He said gravely:

'I don't blame you. I know I didn't give you much of a life.'

'It wasn't the life, Lance. It was you I wanted.'

'I know that, too. It – it was in the cave . . . I was waiting to die. Everything seemed suddenly futile. Except you. Did I make you very unhappy?'

'Yes.' She was sparing him nothing. 'You made me want someone else.'

'Did you find him?'

'Yes.'

'Did you . . . ?'

'Yes.'

'Oh!'

The word came out on a long whisper of weariness. He closed his eyes again and lay back on the pillow, his head turned away from her. He asked dully:

'Do I know him?'

'It was Neil Adams.'

'I should have guessed that.'

'He saved your life when he could have let you die.'

'I suppose I should be grateful.' There was no anger in his voice, only a dull recognition of fact. 'Why are you telling me now?'

Her eyes were still closed so that she could read nothing of his feelings, but she went on, calm and unhurried, piecing out the theme she had lived and dreamed for days and sleepless nights.

'Because I've learnt something, Lance – and I think it's important to both of us. You can't live in this country with a lie. Even if you live alone, you've got to face the truth or go mad because the lie festers up and eats at you like a tropical ulcer. When you've heard me through you may not want me any more. I can take that. I'll go away and start a new life of my own. If you do want me, just as I am, I'll stay and try to make you a good wife, and build you a good property. But not with a lie, Lance. Not with a hate buried somewhere in either of us. We've got to look at each other and see everything, the good, the bad, the failures, the virtues, and say: "I'll take it, just as it stands!" No recriminations, no afterthoughts! If we come together again I want to try to have a child. If we can't make one of our own, I want to adopt one and rebuild our love around it.'

'Do you think you can, after all this?' His eyes were still closed. There was no more animation in his voice.

'I don't know. I've got to be honest about that too.

200

I think it's possible, I think we need to try, both of us. Everybody makes mistakes. The lucky ones make them before they're married and start fresh from there. Others spend their lives regretting the mistakes they didn't make – and that's a kind of lying too. People like us – what do we do? Throw it all down the drain and start again? Or take a good long look at the truth and admit that every man's got a streak of the beast in him and every woman a touch of the tart.' For the first time her voice wavered and the tears began prickling at her eyelids. 'I can't say it any other way, Lance. I've used up all the words. I'm sorry, deeply sorry. But I'm not going on being sorry all my life, with every act and every word a repetition of guilt. I want to live again and laugh, and sing sometimes and go to bed happy. There's a bit of the whore in me. And more than anything else, I want to be able to say one day: "I love you" . . . and to hear you say it to me. That's all, Lance. . . . If you'd like some time to think, I'll go away and . . .'

'No, Mary!' His hands reached out across the coverlet and caught at her wrist. She looked up and saw that his eyes were open. They were grave and hurt, but not bitter. He said soberly:

'I don't know if it will work any more than you do. But a man who's come back from the dead like I have, ought to know the value of what he's got. I'm hurt, shamed too. I'll admit it. If I weren't tied to this bed, I'd take you out and thrash you . . . and Mister bloody Adams too. But even while I was doing it, I'd know you were a better man than both of us, Mary Dillon!

I need you, girl, more than I ever did. I'm no damn good to any other woman. Maybe it's a rough justice that you should be saddled with me. I'd – I'd like to give it a try.'

'On those terms?'

A ghost of a grin brightened his sunken eyes.

'I'm too tired to think of any others.' His eyelids drooped and he lay back on the pillows, all the strength drained out of him. They did not kiss. There was no gesture of reunion, but the slight tightening of his grasp on her wrist before he released her. Already he was on the borders of sleep and she was glad for him. Tomorrow would be time enough to care.

She walked out on to the veranda and watched the sun go down, a glory of gold and purple and crimson behind the ramparts of the naked country.